If You Can

JI Daniels

SPUYTEN DUYVIL
New York City

Library of Congress Cataloging-in-Publication Data

Names: Daniels, J. I., author.
Title: If you can / JI Daniels.
Description: New York City : Spuyten Duyvil, [2020] |
Identifiers: LCCN 2020044157 | ISBN 9781952419324 (paperback)
Subjects: LCGFT: Short stories.
Classification: LCC PS3604.A5334 I38 2020 | DDC 813/.6--dc23
LC record available at https://lccn.loc.gov/2020044157

Contents

It sometimes seems impossible to live. Especially in our bodies. Especially in this world our minds have created.

Like Water

Lillian didn't want to collapse into a literal puddle of water, but some things in life are just out of your hands. That's what her father said at least. It didn't last long, the collapse into liquid. Sometimes it was a melting and a quick reformation, sometimes five or ten minutes of slosh. But it was embarrassing. She felt like she could just die of it. Lillian called it "flooding." It didn't just happen when she was swept up or excited or defeated or triumphant. It wasn't only when she was hungry or tired, or furious or ambivalent. She'd had it happen while riding in the passenger seat, and while watching television. She'd had it when her boyfriend was kissing her, and when she was checking her email. Who knows why. Who knows anything.

The doctors didn't know. Lillian went to loads of them, her parents calmly by her side. They took blood and scraped the inside of her cheek. Nothing seemed wrong with her. They didn't understand when she described the annihilation that was the water. They couldn't believe her when she tried to explain the pain of reforming. She said it was like your shins aching when you were still growing, except it was also like holding an M80 in your fist and squeezing the explosion. It was like the creation of the universe, and like suddenly waking up from a dream. So they sampled lumbar fluid from her spine, they took a piece from the nerves in her left pinkie, they biopsied her spleen. They biopsied everything.

"What do doctors know," she said, frustrated.

"They know a lot. More than anyone," her father said. He considered a little. "At least as far as medicine goes."

"They're only 'practicing' medicine," Lillian said, making air quotes. "When are they going to actually *do* medicine?" She'd heard a comedian say this, and it had struck her as true and ridiculous. It infuriated her to think of such a fraud committed upon the world.

"That's not what that means, honey," her mom said. "To practice, in this context, means to apply the method. This is in contrast to theory. Doctors apply medical methods to their patients. They are practicing medicine, as opposed to creating theories of medicine. As opposed to conducting experiments, or writing papers."

Lillian wore an expression and didn't say anything. She didn't point out that she was the experiment. She would be the paper. Her mother and her father held onto each others' hands and looked terrified and worried and bored and close to crying. Lillian could see they were trying to look calm for her, and she didn't know why it made her so angry. Lillian made her face still.

She kept the still face as she lay back and was pushed into the MRI. She kept the face as machines hummed and clicked and the world felt like it was coming down around her. She kept the face as the doctors waited and waited, and the only time she lost it was when she became a puddle of water, flooding the plastic pan that was bombarded with magnetic resonance imaging.

None of this mattered. She kept turning. More and more often. "I like your hair," a doctor told her, and asked her about what she did with it. "It's so beautiful." But that doctor couldn't figure out what was wrong with Lillian, so what was a compliment? What were some pleasant words?

Her mother told Lillian that she was strong. Her father too, and her doctors. She was strong. Is water strong? It can take anything, but only because it is nothing. Slap it and it splatters, drop it and it pours, punch it and it moves around and envelopes your hand. But water is passive. It only responds. Lillian knew that she was water. Powerless to stop herself from being splattered and poured and punched. Able only to exist.

Lillian was sixteen and couldn't drive. Lillian was, like many people, afraid of walking over grates on the sidewalk, the ones where you could see twenty feet below you, some access or another, some entrance to an underworld of pipes and wires and thirty-foot alligators, but for Lillian, the fear wasn't the fall, it was getting lost in all that water. Where it would take her. When she had first melted in a car seat and came back, her reforming molecules had shredded the car seat as her recreated body pushed herself through the weak fibers of the cloth. Lillian's fear was different than anyone else's. Lillian wasn't afraid of her boobs falling out of a tube top. Lillian was afraid of falling out of her clothes entirely. Lillian was afraid of falling through the earth, of destroying car seats, of what the rules of this illness were—when her reforming body would destroy the object, or when the object would win.

"It isn't fair," Lillian said to her father.

Her father didn't say: "No, it's carnival," or: "Life's unfair," or even: "Being miserable builds character," though he had loved those kinds of jokes. Because Lillian was not a normal sixteen year old, her father was not able to be a normal father. They were not a normal family.

Instead, her father nodded his head and Lillian was grateful not to justify some branch or another of unfairness. There was only that moment at the table, where they sat with a cup of coffee and an acknowledgement of the sorrow and tribulation that was her lot, and they nodded and they accepted because they couldn't understand, and they couldn't do anything other than shrug their shoulders and move on until they would one day be put into such a position that moving was an option no longer afforded to them.

At school, Lillian was deluged with sympathy from her peers and teachers that bordered on the reprehensible, given with the underlying belief that she was just doing it to get attention. "It." As if this auto-eradication of solid structure was a stunt. As if she was wearing a pink Mohawk, or had tattooed her face. As if she was fighting in the hallways or raising her hand in class for every single answer. Just another phase.

Her boyfriend bought her a poster of Bruce Lee, black and white, with the martial arts master in fighting stance, urging the reader to "be like water." The teenage boy version of a kitten telling you to "hang in there." It urged the reader to adapt.

He was trying. Trying to be there for a girl he liked in a situation he couldn't understand. He wanted to be useful, to contribute, to be the rock. Lillian could see that. She could see inside of him the fear and caring and uncertainty. He had signed up for kisses and whatever he could get from a girl that he was attracted to, and instead had gotten a mouthful of water that was his girlfriend disappearing, and then reappearing out of nowhere (head-butting him in the process, giving him a bloody nose), and he had gotten hospital visits and an introduction to medical lingo he had no wish to understand, but was guilted into groking anyways.

Lillian couldn't even shower. No chance. That drain, the running water, the dark unknown beyond. When she would have her next episode? She bathed. Her mother never emptied a sink or a tub without calling for Lillian first. This was life now.

When Lillian broke up with him, when she released him of his obligation, she didn't feel better like she had expected. He wept and said that he loved her. She imagined it would be like opening the flood gates, that the pressure would be relieved. When she locked herself in the bathroom, running the water in the sink and staring at her red and wet face, her mother knocked lightly on the door, and told Lillian that she was proud of her. Her daughter was growing up, and Lillian had made a kind choice. Through the door she said that she was sorry she had to go through this. She was so goddamned sorry. Lillian didn't say anything, and her mother didn't linger. Lillian was grateful for that. And she was grateful she didn't collapse into a puddle of water until after she had already begun to piece herself together again.

"At this point," Lillian's doctor told her, when the flooding had become regular, and grown increasingly common, "you're really in for the star treatment." But he hadn't said this with a sense of irony. He seemed to think that the attention Lillian derived was a kind of compliment. She was flown around the country and interviewed by dozens of doctors and therapists (perhaps it was psychosomatic?) and nurses and aides, and physicists and marine biologists and exorcists. There were so few cases of the illness, and none exactly like hers. Lillian had a few "seats" custom made for her. They doubled as liquid containers. It was as comfortable as it sounded. Lillian sloshed around the country, as maybe only Keith Richards had before, if not in the form of water, exactly.

They began to form a pattern. Each new specialist was professional, but excited. They had heard, but—. Here was the gauntlet to test their mettle, to prove themselves. Lillian at first just couldn't wait to be done with this. But every doctor lost that look of the hero about to succeed. It grew tiresome to watch the doctors wither under her mother's sharp questions, to see them look to her father for help and realize in his gaze that they were alone in that room. Lillian always came back undiagnosed, barely contained.

"What's wrong with you?" well-meaning people would say to her when they found out that she had been sick. If she had forgotten to take off her medical bracelet, people on the street would point at it and ask "what's wrong with you?" Her old schoolmates, the ones she didn't care about, that she didn't update, or talk to, not on Snapchat or Facebook or text or anything, would send her messages out of the blue: "U havnt been in scool, Wats rong w u?"

She ignored them out of principle. Her friends asked too, however they could. And these she ignored because it hurt to even consider the answer.

In the hospitals, the other patients would nod their heads and say, "So what's wrong with you?" And Lillian felt a little like she was home. This was their perverse college, their expensive education. She would tell them how she was messed up, and tell them about the failed tests and the ridiculous questions. She would complain about the phlebotomists that couldn't find a vein if it were their job, and they would tell their own stories. She became an old hand, and would nod at the newbies coming in and say, "So what's wrong with you?" and would see in their faces the light that turned on, that understanding of tone and response that meant they were finally understood.

Eventually, Lillian met a boy that turned into goo, a girl that turned into a smoldering fire (what kind of seat did they use for her?), a woman that collapsed into liquid hydrogen, a man that was a pile of sand. They wondered why they had spent so long believing that they were alone. They exchanged notes. They formed a little clique among the hallways of the ill and infected. Like the X-Men in a depressing alternate reality where heroics were substituted with bedpans. They were glad not to have to spend time with the cancer patients or on the cystic fibrosis floors. To hear about another's disease separates you, even when you're in a similar boat in the same ocean. You find yourself feeling helplessly at a loss. Feeling sorry. When everyone was suffering similarly though, you just knew. You just understood.

The doctors understood that the dissolvers were all the

same, that they were all suffering from the same condition, expressing it differently. If understood was the right word. The doctors insinuated through a probe of questions that the dissolvers were doing it on purpose. Not at first, not when those professionals still imagined they had an idea of what it might be, or a guess; not when they were hopeful of pinpointing the genetic expression, or chemical interaction. But when that failed (and it failed and failed), they would get exasperated, and begin asking questions about diet, about habit, about thought, about feelings, about fashion—questions that never said it directly, but which got the point across. "Why are you doing this," the doctors were saying, though really they were thinking, "why are you doing this to me?"

Lillian's father wasted away. He ate, but it didn't seem to matter. His eyes drooped, his performance at work dissolved. His boss pulled him aside and said that it had to end, that they were sorry and he had their condolences, but he had to get it together. He was going to quit while they still had time together, but Lillian's mother wouldn't let him. His was the good insurance, the insurance that still kept them away from insane copays. He had to persevere. Lillian's mother refused to waste into a shell. She paid the bills and she kept the family together. She didn't let Lillian get away with her outbursts or exclamations, she chastised and punished, even if she were more generous with favors and less strict about the exact definitions of the rules than before the flooding commenced. She always talked about the future. She even sounded like she believed it.

Lillian's mother only wept when no one else could see her, when she thought they couldn't hear. She sat down in the shower and let her body heave against the porcelain. Then she washed her hair, she washed her body, she toweled off and put herself together and came out to hold her family together, broken and frayed: hold them in the semblance of a family.

Lillian did what she could. "You've got to get it together, dad," she would say, and then she would collapse into a puddle. When she returned, she would laugh and laugh and laugh. It barely even hurt anymore, when her body would pull itself into impossibility and then back into bones and sinew and brain. By then, the only thing that hurt was the way she was killing her parents, and the way her mind no longer instantly dismissed the concept of her own mortality.

The sand man went first. Or remained? Lillian couldn't say if he were dead, or what. One day he turned into that pile of beach stuff and just stayed that way. Just a shape in the bed, all over the sheets, spilling onto the floor. Housekeeping had to be banned from the room, their good-intentions of just-doing-their-job becoming a distress to the family having to deal with their loved one being swept into a dustpan with the casual air of tidying a kitchen.

It was when the fire girl went out that Lillian became afraid. With Sandy, the state seemed more like a very-long episode. Like he was just dormant, and would spring back any day now. Any day. Then the girl, her friend, collapsed into smoldering, which dissolved into embers and finally became cold, grey ashes. A dead fire. Her container turning from an adapted bed to a discarded pit, the bonfire a memory, reminiscences of warmth already beginning to fade, remaining only as aching.

"They had names," said Lillian's father, but Lillian didn't say anything to that. She just said Sandy and Smokey, Sandman and Firepit, Beach and Ember. And she cried. Everyone had a name and then they died and it didn't matter anymore, did it?

Goo guy was still alive, though. The frozen girl. Lillian. The doctors doubled down on their attempts. "Kanye West ain't got nothin' on me," she told the "star treatment" doctor, but he had moved on from his bad joke and didn't get the reference. Lucky him, he would get to move on from everything, Lillian realized. The only thing the doctor worried about was that he might have missed something that would become obvious in hindsight. We're both afraid, Lillian thought. He's afraid of being embarrassed. I'm afraid of dying. It's like we're twins.

She wanted to say that to her dad, there was a time he would have liked that joke, but he was already so thin. A skeleton animated by a shoddy stop-motion process. Instead, Lillian changed her tactics, best to revisit the classics. "What do doctors know?" she said.

Her father raised his hands weakly, let them cascade back to his side. "Who knows," he said. "Who?"

Lillian ran back to her old friends, the other kids in the hospital. The ones with the –isms and –imias, who coughed and puked and didn't ever lose corporeal form. It was too much to watch her fellows get swept away, one by one. Lillian needed the separation of a disease that wasn't hers. She wanted to be drowned by the death of a friend without knowing that it is waiting for her too, just around the next corner. What age is too early to foresee your own demise? She didn't ask herself that question and her parents could never have imagined it.

Her parents would say that Lillian had thrived. She had connected with a community. She had found her peace. They would even believe it. They had to.

Lillian's parents wouldn't survive this though. Without their daughter, like water, they splattered, rolling down different angles of the hill that is grief. They would learn to live again, to function and to love. They would connect with others and create new lives for themselves. Not for years, not until they had wallowed in pain without precident, but they would. Just not the same, not together, not with a living daughter.

The other two lived. The one who turned into goo, the one who was liquid hydrogen. There is a movie about their struggles, and Lillian is a supporting character, the sarcastic one who doesn't quite make it, but who gives them the will to keep fighting. Her last words in the film involve her pointing to a picture of Bruce Lee, you know the one, the one where he's in that master's stance, and she exorts them, this movie-Lillian, to "be like water," if you can believe that shit.

Startled Poet Who is a Bat

I was planning to visit with Missus Palm and her five lovely daughters for the rest of the evening, when Modest Swagger, my next-door neighbor and friend by default knocked on the door. This was when I was thirteen, before cell phones were really a thing, if you can believe that, when proximity mattered in a way that seems quaint today. When you were by yourself, you were well and truly isolated.

I could tell that his dad had come home by the cubist rearrangement of Modest's face. His father had a temper like the lust of Zeus, and the consequences were as permanent as they were unpredictable. I fired up the oven and tossed an entire bag of Totinos onto a baking pan that could have used a more thorough cleaning.

After we'd scalded our mouths, and figured out that not even the TV possessed the answers to our teenage malaise that night, Modest told me about the new lady in town who had sequestered herself halfway up the hill. He'd heard that she was some sort of monster. I didn't want to spend my night gawking at strangers, but I still couldn't figure out what to say to Modest's reconfigured face, and so I agreed to the expedition up the dark mountain, down a path that wove its way through clusters of trees that embodied the gruesome versions of medieval fairytales, full of death and witches and bears.

If I could go back to that night, I would tell Modest how the cruelty of our parents is the worst of the pain that we will suffer, for some of us at least, and I would tell him how I couldn't imagine what it was like to have a dad, especially his dad—but we were at least free to head into the darkness of the night. That we had only ourselves and the horror of the rest of our lives ahead of us. This was a blessing, even though it came through suffering. I would have told him that I was hurting too and maybe just being friends was enough for us to survive adolescence. My therapist tells me it is not worth my time to imagine such conversations, though. He tells me that the way forward is simply to practice new behaviors instead of rehearsing old failures. He tells me that even if the thought had occurred to me, I can only say it out loud now because of the twenty years that have passed in reflection. I tend to ignore this advice, and he sighs and admits that most people do.

Modest led me up to the old Humblebreck place, and it was as Gothic a horror as could exist in this nowhere Montana hellscape that was our hometown. It had been built back when the twentieth century was still getting on with it, the last gasp of wealth by a once-prestigious name before they squandered their future in chasing tourists that would never come. Or that would come, decades later, only because of that failure, only because of that beautiful desolation. Hell, I knew, is the place you are trapped, and anywhere is hell when you are a teenager. The house was three stories tall, and as beautiful as it was dilapidated, meeting in that liminal space of nightmares. It was lit up like a beacon, and as we approached, Modest began to tell me about how the Humblebrecks used to own the town, how they owned the towns around us too, and how they had cracked the back of the economy just as surely as Bane had broken Bruce Wayne. I knew the stories too, even though my family had not felt the sting of the fall that the Swaggers had.

We were there, standing in the dark of the woods that crept up near the house, the front door only thirty feet away from the tree line, and I was confronted with the realization that I didn't have a clue what we would do once we arrived. Maybe I didn't think that Modest was telling the truth, or maybe I did, maybe I was complicit, and have conveniently forgotten that part of my history.

Modest began throwing rocks, small ones, and I joined in. We peppered the front of the house with gravel, one slag at a time, and then in handfuls, the small grey stones falling against the peeling paint and windows like a rainstorm, coming in sheets. We circled, grabbing bigger rocks and pelting the house, the sound growing to the crack of thunder, the dark of the night swallowing us. Inside, we could see the woman. At first, she only peered out into the darkness, but then, as we increased the size of the rocks, she fled, flittering around inside the house, the light catching her, showing us her bat-wings, and she was just as Modest had told me, and I began to think that maybe everything he had ever said must be true.

I like to think that Modest started shouting first, but

even if he did, I was soon joining him, screaming, throwing, running, our bodies a teenage ecstasy. As my voice grew raw, I realized I was shaking. I realized that I was as alive as I had ever been. We called her rat-wing and blood-sucker. We called her leaf-nose and bug-eater and blind-eyes and guano. We told her we were here to shove a stake in her heart and we were here to burn down her house and we were pest control and we were INS here to send her back to Transylvania.

We aimed for the glass. When we missed, the house would clap and shudder. When we hit, the windows erupted in crystalline applause.

I threw a rock the size of a grapefruit that smashed into the front door like a battering ram. We could see that it would give way to our might and our power and our control if only we kept it up. Modest and I found the biggest rocks we could throw and we hurled them with our arms and our shoulders and our hearts. If we could only destroy this door, we would destroy everyone that was holding us back, and we would destroy the lives of our oppressors, we would destroy oppression entirely. Our fathers and our no-fathers would cease to even be a concept. We would no longer have to live in fear because fear would be eradicated, and all that would be left is opportunity, and we wouldn't have to be next-door neighbors because we would be getting out of here and we would be the people we were meant to be, which was good and kind and smart and successful, and we would look back upon our days with horror and an ironic knowledge that what is behind will always taste sweet and the future will always be an unknown, and we would know then that we should have lived our lives in the present, because every awful moment was building us into the men we were truly meant to be.

When we ran out of the rocks that were like grapefruits, Modest picked up one that was a volleyball, and he charged the door, his face twisted into a cruel ecstasy, ready to finish the job that a dozen lobbed stones had started. The woman inside flipped on the lights, and she threw open the front entrance with the force of bad news and she was holding a gun that existed for this very reason, and there was only a moment when Modest and the woman both understood what was happening, when they both understood that it was out of their control, that everyone had played their hands and all that was left was the reckoning.

*

Did you know that when you are covered in blood that is not yours and your mind is not yours either, that a wing, wrapped around you while the Sheriff makes the two-hour drive, is like a silk hammock? I don't remember any other details of that night, and I am told that this is a response to trauma. I have chosen to forget because it was too much for me. It was the evidence of my actions, brought to a head. I can only remember that touch.

I remember her face. I saw it much later, in the light of a tiny courtroom, and it was so small, like a deer's face, her eyes big and kind and not at all what I would have expected. She did not look back at me. I would find out that she was a writer, that a friend of hers had told her about this place, way out in nowhere, where the people were kind, where the skies were endless, and where the isolation was an analgesic for women like her. Her name was Samantha, and she was trying to find a place that was far from the life that she had lived, and away from the kinds of "good boys" that wound up finding her anyways.

I wrote her a letter a long time ago. She never responded. I found her online since then and she is alive, thriving out in Sweetwater. It is sad, but I can't think of anything that has made me happier than that news. Not for a long time. I want to tell her that I am sorry, but I've already surprised her when she thought she was safe, and I don't want to come out from the woods into her light, light that shines out against the darkness, to give her my message. Not again.

The Boxes

So a stockbroker had killed himself in a particularly gruesome fashion. Or that's how the security door chatter went. No one seemed to know details, only the severity. Shawna and Eric found that it was hard to care very much for a stockbroker, especially when his untimely demise meant that the apartment came so *cheap*.

"It's sad, you know?" Some neighbor prattled on, while Shawna and Eric made appropriately conciliatory nodding movements.

"Used to bring in boxes by the armload," said the doorman. "Always some new gadget or chaise. Sold his old stuff on the cheap." And the doorman nodded sagely at that, appreciative, of course, for the dead fool who spent money so easily and discarded his remnants, nearly new. It was difficult to tell if the doorman admired the money it took, or if he simply missed the opportunity.

"We keep a kind of a lifestyle here," said the manager of the building, a woman who smelled of exorbitant perfume and rancid memories. "Stay fashionable, don't hold onto the past. Right? It's a new world every day."

Shawna and Eric kept nodding and smiling their plasticine grins at the manager with her thick vertical stripes fighting a hopeless battle with perception, and made their way through the paperwork. Eric was an Art Director, Shawna a Lawyer; they understood. They had the bank evaluate their assets, they put down the twenty percent, they hired contractors to poke and prod at the space to assure that there were no ashboring beetles in the pine studs, that their drywall wasn't damp.

They signed documents, gathered notaries and priests, and did the usual necessaries. They agreed to monthly payments that could send a less fortunate human to a good school; their firstborn was promised to the house of R'lyeh, should it arise within their lives; they promised to pay the appropriate Federal, State, County, City, Municipal and Girl Scout cookie taxes; they swore never to wear white after labor day, except on occasion of a mid-winter white-tie event among the snowdrifts; they made a pledge not to hoard money, agreeing to stimulate the economy with judicious fashion choices and injudicious credit card debt. They also agreed to always carry insurance on the apartment for fire, theft, flood and shag carpet. They did all of the above under penalties of jail, wrist slapping, death and dismemberment, the sacrifice of their lives (and souls) to feed the complex Golem, an extra day of Lent, six more weeks of winter and up to—and including— social shunning at work related parties.

*

The price for an apartment in Tribeca is based on an exponential calculation of the square footage. One fourteenth of their current mortgage would have afforded them a small working airport in Omaha, with a hanger for each of their outfits and a maintenance shed for shoes, but they knew how to make sacrifices. The blood of a stockbroker can only reduce rent prices so far. They wanted more space, but they would manage, Eric had thought, until he and Shawna watched the movers unload shrink-wrapped furniture into the corners of each room, stacking their boxes into enormous Hopewell mounds in the center.

"This is too much," they said, preparing their offerings to the gods of the Chaco Canyons, in penance for their hubris. They had cut back, donated, gifted, sold, recycled and trashed what must have been ten thousand cubic feet of their lives before hurling themselves across the country—they thought this would be enough. Wasn't it enough? They had tithed in clothing, electronics, and particleboard, so that they would be saved. Saved this moment.

Shawna wielded her sharpie, Sikanda, which only those who have bathed in the flames of death can bear the brunt of, and made another pass, slashing a dark emblem on that which would not survive this second round. And so they winnowed their Home Depot® boxes, attempting to curb the height of the towering masses. It was futile. What had been a neat (if terrifying) pile, sank into a cacophony of clutter as objects with no place to go began a slow, disorganized crawl, littering the tiers of boxes, sapping any further plans to unpack.

They collapsed onto their mattress that night, the bed a disorganized mess of jumbled RealWood© shoved to the corners of the room, the boxes moved from their polyhedronal shape in the center to cancerous masses in the corners. Their lamps were still packed three piles deep, and so they gazed in that darkness at the general direction of the other, their apartment so gloriously high above the huddled masses that even the streetlights of New York City couldn't penetrate their windows.

"We'll be fine, right?"

"We'll be fine."

"But the boxes are still there. What if they fall? What if a criminal gazes through the window with a drone, sees our entire home, boxed for the taking? What if our sacrifice was not enough?"

"We gave enough. More than enough. We purged."

"We did. We weeded, we cut, we trashed, we burned. We are free to travel, to gain more. It's why we're here, after all. We are light."

"We are lightness itself. We are angels."

They slept, at last, and did not stir. Their minds did not flicker with concern as the nebulous shape in the corner of their room blossomed a little, multiplied.

*

There was no space even to unload, for the boxes were infinite, their far edges gaping into the maw of the universe where heat death was already spreading; and they were crammed: with a bread machine, mechanical pencils, a single woman's sock that Shawna didn't recognize, and with marital aids. Eric and Shawna would have to buy more furniture to even think of dealing with the mess. They donated the marked items and headed to the shopping district. Storage was the key, and so they wandered warehouses with pallet loaders at bay to examine one-offs and knockoffs of every conceivable style. Pottery Barn®, Ikea®, Ashley Furniture®, Crate and Barrel®, The

Container Store®, Pier One®, Target®, Wal-Mart® even. Everywhere. The only way to reduce what you have is to buy something new to contain it.

They loaded their rented U-Haul® pickup truck— they were not the sort to deal in open-backed vehicles normally—until the pile was as tall as the cab, strapping down the payload with bungie cords and hair scrunchies, inching their way home to spend the evening assembling the new furniture, arranging it, collapsing the material into piles for recycling: here cardboard, here plastic, here Styrofoam and twist ties, here the shoelace for a loafer Eric had never owned. They were such very good citizens.

Shawna and Eric surveyed their land, made new with storage solutions, with furniture and clear bins, with under bed pull-outs and cubes hanging from the closet. The pile in the corner was slightly reduced. They went to bed that evening delighted.

"You see? We gave, and so we get."

"We gave so much. Half a truckload it must have been. A quarter, at least."

"I almost wished we could have saved it. Repaired the chips, buffed the scratches, kept it close. To lose an item is to lose a limb, I think."

"'The more stiches, the less riches,' as they say."

*

But their work was not done, for in the morning, the building manager "Just popped by to say hello," took a look at the stacks of boxes and let them know that this would not suffice. They expected a certain standard of living. Eric and Shawna assured her that it wasn't what she thought, shuffled her out of the apartment with the shooing motions reserved for gnats and persistent investors, and continued to unload their storage containers and storage-friendly furniture. They pulled out their fondue pots and cheese boards, the cheese platters and cheese knives, the fondue sticks and fondue-stick-friendly bowls. They pulled out their icecream maker.

"I thought I threw this out."

"It's perfectly fine, I un-threw it out."

"It's not fine. We discussed this."

"Oh god."

"The icecream comes out too hard."

"That's the fault of the chef, of the recipe, not of the tool. It's perfectly fine."

"The new model has a nitrogen injection nozzle. Instant, fluffy, frozen delight."

"This is ridiculous. We're keeping it."

They fought about the life they should be living and what this old/perfectly-fine machine represented, but then decided to just marinate in their discontent, quietly. They fermented it, letting out the compressed air in long, loud, sighs. They returned to the boxes, which had grown above them, nearly touching their ten-foot ceilings, leaning precariously over their heads. As shelves were filled with decorative books and dumbbells were strategically placed in locales where they could be seen (but barely) by guests—each placement made with irritated resignation—the towers above wobbled, and both Shawna and Eric were struck with the debris from a dislodged box of marital aids.

"What's this?"

"You know exactly."

It wobbled as they argued, vaguely translucent, a color

that might be called flesh, but more accurately was what a poorly passing android might be slathered in. "I told you I don't like this. I wanted it gone."

"You're just insecure."

"Who wouldn't be? That it even resembles what it claims to be is unnerving. How are we ever supposed to even touch each other when this monstrosity lurks in our closet, waiting for me to step out of the house?"

The conversation escalated. Words were used that had no place in the dialogues of intimate partners. Words like: kookaburra, asparagus, infinitesimal, casserole, buffalo, and string-theory. Détente was not reached, only a future fight ensured, when the offending item was re-boxed and added back to the still-growing pulsating pile in the corner.

*

In line for a brunch cramburger (of course, a hamburger obscenely slid into a cronut), the nice man who lived below them, who wore Hawaiian shirts with incredible sophistication and reading glasses like a child, told Shawna and Eric that the building manager was horrible, but she had the best intentions. Things are memories, he explained, our past personified. Who needed that weighing us down? He recalled how he had loved his Cannon® Rebel XTi™, with its thirteen hundred megapixel prowess, and pristine quality, that he could load onto his 128GB PNY Elite Performance® SDXC memory card to take thirteen pictures of every interesting thing, then store on his Dell® Opteron™ Workstation©/∞ for a few years before just throwing that whole thing away and starting new. Because who wants to look at how much hair you didn't have anymore, or how much skinnier you aren't?

"Who are we, if not our pasts?" Eric asked.

And the neighbor in his bright shirt shrugged and said "Americans," before leaving them. His turn in line was up.

The cronuts were flaky, sugary, delicious, but overrated. The burger weighed it down, undid what was good about the pastry. It was a bad pairing. Unlike, Shawna and Eric had gathered, the ramen burger down the street. Now that was supposed to be something special. The thing about fusion, they overheard someone saying in line, is that it takes a cuisine, strips it of its history, and makes it something that is even better than new. It makes it into something that is trending. A trend is better than new. New is better than history. That which is ethereal is more precious, right?

*

At their apartment, the boxes were now twelve feet tall at their lowest ledges, the space where box and ceiling met was a Klein bottle of despair. A box descended outside of the bounds of gravity and opened its flaps like a flower opening for the dawn, full of old greeting cards that Eric and Shawna had once exchanged.

"We need to toss this."

"How can we? Remember how romantic these were?"

"Remember how cheesy? How tedious? We need to purge. We need to move on."

"Of course you want to move on. It's been ages since you've been romantic."

"Like you were better. Here, let's read one of your love poems." And Shawna grabbed a piece of paper she knew she didn't write. "'For the secret one/The one of darkness and of night/ The one who comes when dawn is near/ And brings me to the light.' I don't remember this."

"Where did you get that?" It wasn't possible. He knew that. He'd held this poem in his hand, shaking, tears in the corner of eyes, and put it to the flame, held it upright so that only the barest corner had escaped, and that had been buried in the dirt.

Even a clueless spouse doesn't need much more than a brief, unfiltered look of terror and wonder in the eyes of the caught, a vacuum that is suddenly filled with a new look of profoundly innocent bafflement.

"Everything," Shawna said, her voice a croak, "everything must go."

"It didn't mean anything." It was the script of an argument they weren't having.

Who even cared what it had meant? "It doesn't matter. Nothing stays. I'll burn it if I must." And Shawna began to move the boxes to the door as she called the movers that had been unsubtly suggested by the manager. "It's an emergency," she said on the line. Instantly, they were there. They began to pick up the boxes and to haul them away.

"No," Eric said, "we need to talk about this."

"There's nothing to talk about. Let's look forward, let's move ahead. You want me to forget about that letter, don't you?"

"Yes."

"Let's forget everything." The boxes quivered in anticipation.

"No," Eric said, knocking a box from her arms. "This is our history. It is important." Out spilled an M&M® wrapper, then a whole horde of them, every single package that Eric had ever eaten. Out spilled the membership to Gold's Gym™ where he first ran into the writer of that poem. Here was the torn Trojan® foil, here was the receipt for the Four Seasons®. It was no longer even a surprise to see the catalog of his failures.

Shawna ignored the outpouring, carried armful after armful of boxes to the door, where movers, like ants, were already beginning to stream.

Eric, stricken, could only lash out. He yelled at the movers but they said nothing, ignoring him, the snake of their line winding around his pinwheeling body. He managed to pull a box from their hands. It crashed to the ground and spilled its contents across the floor, a tidal wave of brown cubes, each containing a box as big as, or bigger, than the one that had come before it, each filled with emails and handwritten notes from Lehman Brothers; binders of toxic assets and terminally unwise lending decisions, transcriptions of hushed meetings in which executives skirted regulations.

Another box burst open, containing one hundred and ten thousand orders of internment in Topaz for those men and women and children who had dared to be born Japanese in a time of war. Below these files, in the same box, with a bottom that was endless, the medical records of the Tuskegee experiments.

Another box. Addressed from Fort Pitt: a pile of blankets.

Another. An assortment of letters, with topics that centered around the Children of Ham, and how, it could be argued, this was simply the will of God.

Another. A gun, a knife, a noose. Agent Orange™ and a car battery in a pool of water. A pyramid of hooded humans, a shovel, a camera, a *New York Times* article. A nuclear warhead, mustard gas and credit card statements.

Around Eric, the room had emptied almost entirely. Like a magic trick. There was only him, the box, Shawna, the manager lady in her bulging stripes. "We have to hold onto something, we have to remember or else we will repeat—" he said, but said nothing further, because the box swallowed him whole. Shawna took the knife and slid it through the side of the cardboard with a pink noise and the last of the movers removed it to be incinerated with everything else.

"It was the only way," said Shawna.

"We'll find you another," said the manager, her face grotesque and smiling. "This is New York. There's always something else, something better. A doctor, a lawyer, a Senator. And there is this apartment, restored to its true glory."

It was warm, the summer afternoon drowsy with the buzzing of ABC7 Eyewitness News®copters and the fainter drone of United® jets passing thousands of feet overhead, like a caress on the soft air. Shawna drew a deep breath, gazing across the living room out through the veranda into the round blue horizon.

"Isn't it beautiful!" Her voice trembled a little. "Simply perfect for a chaise lounge."

Now or Never or Later

We drove straight on. The temperature in Lincoln, Maine was so cold the dirt from the backhoe came out onto the icy snow in broken brown sheets like ceramics fired in freeze. We left that behind along with our responsibilities, the color black and face nets. We fled down I-95 with such velocity it may have seemed we were a confused bird making a too-late retreat to the south. We were headed to Oceanside, California to stare at the Pacific until, thirteen miles out, our gaze would be swallowed by the sea.

The shoulder was the dirty white of nearly perpetual snow, the highway the color of melting and drying salt mixed with miniscule flakes of rubber. The trees were dead and the cities we passed seemed in an eternal depression; still-inhabited ghost towns. We wished for warmth.

By the time we merged onto I-90 west, the temperature had risen to a balmy freezing and the heavens opened for a medley of rain, hail and sleet the purview of Chicken Little. The only sound in the car was the sonorous hum of rubber and cement meeting, sending sound and vibration like texture through the car, and the roar of the WRX's boxer engine. The radio had died months before and conversation was not on our mind. Drivers changed when the monotony of being a passenger became too much. Some find driving to be the tiresome activity, but we dreaded the listless window watching and intermittently napping of the unoccupied passenger. Sometimes, when the drone of engine and friction grew unbearable, we rolled down the windows and let winter rip through the car, snow and all, with a roar that eased our minds and sent our long hair into convulsions like Medusa's snakes ready to strike.

Outside of Syracuse, after filling up on gas, we spotted a hitchhiker huddled over his duffle bag near the ramp onto the highway. We exchanged looks and in our glazed eyes there was consensus. When he yanked open the back door, our dollar coffees in jumbo Styrofoam cups steamed the suddenly frigid interior. Whorls of snow entered and were annihilated upon touching anything, as if everything with us was antimatter. He gave his thanks and tossed the green canvas duffle across the seat like a corpse and crawled in. He asked us where we were heading and we told him west. The question was how far, but when we answered that we were going as far as John Soul would have approved of, our passenger disappeared into the quiet of personal reflection. We didn't mind.

After a few minutes of empty, purgatorial silence, the hitchhiker told us he was heading to Seattle to start a grunge band, though we could drop him in Pennsylvania, at his aunt's, if we grew tired of him. He laughed at his sensible humor. He told us he knew what we were thinking, that he was thirty years late for a grunge band, but wasn't that the glory of the plan? He wanted no big label, no Nirvana sell out, he would hawk his audio wares via the internet, a song at a time and who would take him seriously in that cyber space if his IP was located in bumfuck, New York? He leaned forward from the backseat when he talked, alternating his voice between us, like we were a rapt audience and he was wont to neglect either of us of his gaze. We nodded as if we understood and he smiled and leaned back.

We passed an hour in relative quiet, the loquacious hitchhiker trying now and then to engage us in small talk, but we were disinclined. Each time the conversation keeled, though, he attempted to resuscitate it. He told us his name was Clark Araxie but that he goes by Kent, the reasons being two: his hatred of his given name and his love of a pun. When he paused to allow us the frame of time to introduce ourselves, we said nothing and then when he opened his mouth and let it hang, unsure of whether to prod for more, we said it was a pleasure to meet you, Clark, and left it at that.

Outside, the snow, modulating in size and frequency like the emotional states of a suicide pact, began to fall more heavily, the cold solidified into cotton white tufts. We lost speed as the dimming day's cloud harvest caught the beams of light from the car, illuminating each separate flake, cutting visibility to shreds and guestimations. Clark pontificated about the beauty of nature, of snow and of gravity. He explained his conception of string theory as gleaned from mass market paperbacks and the necessity for good grunge bands. He told us how they were connected, or how they should be. He spoke until his logic was a tightly wound ball of thread entirely unwound, then stuffed into a small bag and shaken. He segued into a mild rebuke, flirtatiously cautioning us on the danger of driving in such weather, we should have known better; though he was thankful for the ride. We told him to shut up, both craning our necks to stare at him until he nervously suggested we might, maybe, watch the road? We drove the car faster into the Ganzfeld until we could hear our passenger's knuckles turning bloodless.

Within an hour, Clark decided that he should pay respects to kin and drop by his aunt's house after all. Through the rearview mirror, in the gloaming before dark fell in earnest, we watched him hike down the offramp towards Erie. We laughed at Clark/Kent and the shedding of our unplanned visitor lightened the evening. We must have been scary to send him into the cold like that, we said, and we proposed ways in which we were terrifying. We were women without a man, without lipstick and mascara; we were women left the house, unafraid of hitchhikers; we were women who didn't know to be thankful of musicians and small talk; we were women and not girls or chicks or babes or girlfriends or wives. Perhaps it was our driving. It was a shame, we said, that we never even got to show him our hair whipped up in the wind, and wouldn't that have been something to really give him a fright, maybe he would have been frozen into lifeless stone, for hadn't we also been beautiful once?

It snowed through Pennsylvania and Ohio and Indiana and Illinois as we flew across I-80 with the swiftness of a horror movie's almost-victim. The one who wouldn't go until much later. We held the steering wheel at ten and two and the passenger helped guide the driver as we made headway through the wanting visibility. As we came into Iowa, the sun was glowing on the horizon, the light a cracked egg yolk yellow, spreading across a skillet. The snow relented to a frozen aspersion. The ground was too warm, the winter too mild for anything to stick and so we ignored the speed limit signs entirely and let the car hurtle across the flat landscape.

The snow never quit and we talked of falling. We remembered plane crashes, parachute incidents, building implosions and the Bermuda triangle. We recalled the woman who had leapt from the Space Needle, parachute in hand, to prove that base jumping was safe. She plunged over five hundred feet. Onlookers recalled with horror how they watched her struggle, kicking and squirming in vain to straighten the lines of her chute. When she landed in the wet grass, she bounced. Didn't she? We didn't remember, but what we did remember was that she lived. She broke her back, but only a little bit. Maybe she only bounced back, maybe the word didn't mean that her body had compressed and released to such a degree that she was flung, ever so briefly, back into the air before falling again; maybe it was just a metaphor. We hadn't known before then that you could break your back just a little bit.

The cop flipped his lights on as we passed, but at our velocity they quickly winked out of sight behind us. We pretended we had not seen the patriot strobe and it took five minutes for the law to overtake us. We pulled over and prepared license, registration and proof of insurance, handing them over as we rolled down the window. The trooper took the papers and examined them, peering into the car at our faces and he asked us what we were doing.

Instead of answering the question we told him our parents had died. In the moment of quiet, the tiny flecks of snow that landed and melted on the trooper's hat were fairy tale sparkles in the morning light. The badge on his chest read Conway and was the color of smoked gold. He asked us if were heading to the hospital, but no, we told him we had left the funeral. We were going to a better place. He left us then, and went to his car while we sat in silence and contemplated our fate, our actions; our status in life as we knew it—as orphans. When he returned, the policeman handed us back our information and gave us a look that belied an understanding of sorrow and despair and he implored us to get inside, get something to eat and to obey the speed limit. Freed from punishment, we were unwise enough to ask if that was his advice to all young women, to stay inside and do what they were told. He stared at us for the interval sometimes called a beat before he turned, returned to his vehicle, whipping through the median, back to where he had come from.

It seemed fitting to arrive in Lincoln, Nebraska almost exactly one day into our journey and almost exactly halfway through: from the edge of nowhere to the middle of nowhere. By then the air had warmed to a relatively pleasant thirty four degrees and the puffs of snow had turned instead to a drizzle. The rain steadily increased as we ploughed into Colorado, growing heavier with each small, dark town we passed until each drop was like a spurt from a turkey baster. We navigated the inclines and declines of the mountains. We could only open our windows for moments at a time before we were beaten and soaked by the rain, our hair not so much Gorgon as drowned rat.

At Battlement Mesa we pulled over at a rest area to grab snacks and switch drivers. The rain came down like a nightmare and even though it was only five in the evening it seemed midnight dark. An old trucker named Shannon hovered near the vending machines lamenting the precipitation. We told him it could be worse, it could be snow coming down this hard and then we'd be stuck in a blizzard. We told him that the storm had been following us all the way from Maine but that we would outrun it. He implored us to stay for a little bit, to let the rain subside, like he assumed we were family all seeking shelter from the fat tears of heaven and we could keep each other company. He told us that you can't outrun a storm, it is nature and even if you think you're ahead of it, it can sweep forward suddenly and then where would you be? He tried to convince us that storms didn't even run westward. We ran into the rain and the trucker tried once again to detain us, yelling at our backs that ignoring something wasn't the same as bravery and seeking shelter wasn't domesticity, but by then we were at the car and soaked. Also, we have learned enough in life to distrust anything like folksy wisdom, especially from characters whose hearts may be made of gold. We hopped in and slammed the doors behind us, killing the roar of the rain and turning it into a patter.

Lightning flared in the mountains, despite the cold, and rumbled eternally through the valleys. It wasn't possible of course, except that it was happening. A refrain we understood completely. Aside from the cacophonous illumination we could barely see. The road, dark and wet, took the glare from our headlights and sent it hurtling off the asphalt in a way that made the lonely white dashes nigh invisible. The rain fell so hard it became obvious there were no clouds above, only the grey, leaking bottom of a secret ocean in an expired universe. When the drops hit the ground they did it with so much force that they shattered into particles. It was the type of mist that surrounds a waterfall, the long descent of even water's oblivion. The sound of wetness was a dragon, triumphed over in sound only by the explosions of ionized air—their bright flashes and artillery booms. We were still damp. We were low on gas.

We talked of survivors. We talked of those who had faced the maw of death and had lived to see the cornucopia of life and who had recoiled at it. Holocaust survivors whose lesson learned was that the world is composed of evil persons with evil motives waiting to enact their evil deeds—those who lived and had committed suicide. We discussed those children raised by wolves who were unable to communicate in the human world even as they picked up snatches of language and a barebones of comprehension, but whose native life was gone. We talked of orphans: from Oliver Twist to Dave Eggers. We did not speak of ourselves.

Among the rain and the storm and the night, came again the sounds and sights of a policeman's siren. This time, however, it was not in pursuit of us, our reckless speed was still ten miles under the limit. The cop flew past, disappearing as quickly as it had appeared into the dark and the wet. Not five minutes later, as we passed the town of Hurricane, Utah, the lights passed again, from where it had come. Forward, we continued in the night, the rain falling even harder.

We saw it simultaneously: a river across the road, black and shimmering, the light of our headlights reflecting even more brightly, the marbles of rain sending shimmering waves, a million times a million of them, rippling across its expansive surface. To the right of the flat road was a river gone unnoticed in the weather and ahead was its impromptu tributary, recently sprung from an excess of precipitation and a dip in the road. While the brakes shuddered their mechanical dance of not-locking, the car slid slightly to the right in those two seconds before impact—one Mississippi, two Mississippi.

The Subaru's front end plunged downward, sending a wall of water straight up that landed on our windshield, further blinding us; the wheels sent plumes of spray out each side of the car. Momentum carried us into the middle of the new river before the tires rested on solid ground and motion ceased, finally. But the water pushed from the passenger side, swelling to the level of the window and seeping through the cracks. It was on our feet. It was cold and hostile, murky, smelling of earth and death. A muddy ablution. We punched the gas and the tires spun, moving us a foot forward, but skidding as the stream pushed us three feet to the left. We rocked back and forth, urging the car onward as the tragic diagonal continued, three feet to our loss for every foot to safety. We felt the soft touch of dirt and grass beneath the car as we were pushed off of the road and across the median and the touch of cement again as we drifted past the remaining lanes. The river could only have been twenty feet across but our progress made it seem the Euphrates. Denial is not just a river in Egypt, the joke goes. We bumped over the last lane and the shoulder and onto the grass again where the river-actual waited. We rocked hard and gunned the gas and urged the car forward and for no reason the car ceased its crabwise motion with a thump, its wheels gripping onto a wrinkle of the landscape and lurching those last ten feet out of the water, coming to rest on the side of the road. We had been holding our breath.

I breathed.

Bob Six

Bob Six doesn't think much of Bobs one through five. It's an itch and a scratch problem. The more you scratch, the more it itches. Think of the lover you have laid in bed with, happy and content until you ask them what they're thinking, and they must be pulled back from some deep and engaging reverie in order to mutter an unconvincing "nothing." No good comes from picking at it. No answer will satisfy. All that Bob Six can really do is to rub the balm of disinterest on that particular irritant of curiosity and focus on how the sixth time will surely be the charm.

That's the advice that Mom Three-Fifteen gave him, and it seems sound. Like the kind of wisdom that takes three hundred and fourteen iterations to get quite right.

Bob Six drives a car. He's good at it, and he damned-well should be. He remembers his third birthday, when he began his daily go-cart training. It wasn't much, that training cart, but with a little tinkering he was able to get it up to forty-three on the straightaways. Only Bob Three was ever faster, but everyone knew how well that went for him. Bob

Six likes to think that his secret is predicting the behaviors of cars that have been snuck-up-on from behind, which is good because the entire Allen line had problems with getting sideswiped by surprised civilians.

Margaret Two tells Bob Six that the Allens were a weird little branch that he shouldn't worry about at all, so Bob doesn't.

That's the other thing Bob Six does well. Listen to what he's told. He's not brainless. He knows what's what and what's rot, but the way he figures, it doesn't make much of a difference—because if the boss tells him to do something that's rot and he doesn't do it, the scrapper is the result. Knowing that the Siberian Peninsula is part of Asia and not Europe doesn't change the heat of the biofurnace. Bob Six does sometimes wonder what's the point of calling them separate continents when they're as connected as landmasses really get, but he's more of a wheelman than a Mapologist. He knows that mapologist isn't the right word, but that's the kind of specific information that isn't worth looking up.

Bob Six may be the world's greatest pizza delivery driver, but he still gets yelled at by his boss. Maybe, he thinks, this is because bosses like to yell. Bob Six likes to drive, Mom Three-Fifteen likes to give advice, Boss likes to yell. It gives the world symmetry. Margaret Two says there ain't nothing in the world makes sense. Bob Six is beginning to think that Margaret isn't such a nice person to spend his time with.

Bob Six meets Eva in pretty much exactly the way in which you would expect. She orders a pizza, though she isn't quite home yet, and he beats her there, passing her at eighty-six miles an hour on a one lane road. She pulls into her own driveway only after he's knocked on her door.

If you were to radically simplify Eva's taste for men into two kinds—which you should not do, as this ignores the complexity of human psychology in favor of dramatic statements—she could be said to go for men who have a lurking unease with their lot in life, and men who can thread a needle in a corporate sedan. She invites Bob Six into her house for refreshments, but Bob isn't used to such social cues, declining in order to make time on his next piping-hot pizza delivery.

Eva begins ordering more pizzas. You know the story. She interrogates Bob Six because there is something she needs or wants, but Bob knows that the why is outside his ken. Bob Six is not allowed to own anything, yet he has a hammer and a cat (Persei 8). Bob Six has had three lovers: Margaret Two (a mistake), Aaron Five (a surprise), and Michio Forty-Two (a delight). Bob Six is a driver at heart, not just as a trade, and he has a lust for travel. Bob Six has never seen a bird feed worms and grasshoppers to its chirping babies. He'd like to though.

Eva feels herself falling for Bob Six, and so she does the right thing and buys him from the pizza parlor, which will have to move on to Bob Seven. Besides, she's needed a driver since her latest promotion.

At night, Bob Six prefers his new position much more than his last. Wink wink, nudge nudge, says Margaret Two when he tells her. But during the day there is less to do. Corporate drivers are not allowed the speed limit leeway that delivery drivers are, so he isn't able to get to one-twelve on the straightaways, weaving through traffic like a hummingbird through a field of flowers. But it isn't all bad. There is something to navigating the risk of being caught with the need to go faster. His day is spent largely waiting for Eva to do what she does.

Eva asks Bob Six if he ever wishes that he wasn't owned, and Bob Six has some very complicated feelings about that whole thing—if he couldn't be owned, he wouldn't have been bred, and then how could he have any thoughts on the subject, but also he wondered if—but he tells her no, he doesn't ever wish that, because if he hadn't been owned by his old boss and delivering pizza, then how would he ever have met Eva? Eva's too smart to fall for that, but she does it anyways, because she doesn't want to think about what else he might have said. They will both think about it later, and then drive the thought from their heads, because there are no answers to that question that would let them be happy with their situation.

Besides, Eva says. It isn't like my ex-husband didn't hire himself his own personal Asa Nine from the massage parlor. She says this with a lilt that suggests something Bob Six hadn't considered before.

Bob Seven delivers their pizza. He is always late. Not late, per se, but slower than Bob Six would have been. One day Bob Six tells Bob Seven that he is better than him. Bob Seven cocks his head and tells him that they're the same. Bob Six nearly hits him. He resents Bob Seven, though he denies it to himself. He and Eva begin to eat less pizza.

Bob Six asks Eva what it all means. She sighs and says that she doesn't know. She books them a trip to Italy, where they eat only pizza that is never delivered, that must be slipped directly from the oven into your mouth. Eva makes a joke about Mario 128, but Bob Six does not understand it. When they return, Persei 8 has had kittens and Eva grows wistful. Bob Six knows that this is his fault, but there is nothing he can do about it. Eva says that it isn't his fault. Maragaret Two has been replaced by Margaret Three, who has a somehow worse attitude, and is soon replaced by Margaret Four.

Bob Six asks Mom Three-Sixteen what it all means, and she tells him that it's an itch and a scratch problem, and he's better off just rubbing on a balm of disinterest. Bob Six sees that this is the kind of wisdom that takes three hundred and fifteen iterations of refinement in order to sound like the utter rot it is.

Pillars of Thorns

It was the year the blackberries took over Seattle. They grew from every patch of dirt, crawling over everything, halving the population in a matter of months through mass exodus. From her faraway apartment in North Carolina, smothered in neglected laundry and art supplies, Lisa obsessed, watching the heads of scientists and religious leaders and military spokesmen as they went on talking and the vines of the blackberries went on growing.

It had been a month since her mother's funeral when Lisa's father asked her to meet him for a drink. She wasn't working anyway. She bled vacation time drinking, watching television and reading art magazines. She wasn't returning any of the worried phone calls from her friends, she wasn't painting, *therapeutic creativity* her shrink called it, she wasn't seeing her either. She pulled up her résumé and added *Advent Advertising: Graphic Designer. 6 years* to the previous employment portion. She printed a dozen copies but didn't even staple them. She didn't want to interrupt her self-destruction by meeting her father for drinks but went anyway because she could use some company that wouldn't try to cheer her up.

"Dad," Lisa said, sliding into the seat across from her father. It was two thirty in the afternoon, so the bar was almost empty. He'd grabbed a booth near the window and even though there was a thin white curtain pulled over the glass, the sun filtering in was still nearly blinding.

The bartender made his way to their table and read them the specials that they ignored in favor of a Macallan and water for him, a Sapphire and tonic for her. Lisa squeezed the lime into the liquid and stirred it around with her little straw. Dad was still wearing his wedding ring. She watched the light reflect off of the yellow gold and for a moment it seemed like the brightest light in the bar, but it was just a reflection, the ring the symbol of an expired contract.

"Lisa," he said to her after a while, and then he picked up his untouched drink. He held it in his hand like he was going to make a toast, but set it back down. "I'm moving to Seattle."

Every memory Lisa had was wrapped in Greensboro, playing in the streets around the neighborhood, walks at Lake Daniel Park, University at NC State where her little brother still went to school, her job. She grew up in the house on Carpenter Court. To lose that would be to lose everything she was. "I'll go with you."

"I was hoping you would."

They drank in silence. After a few minutes the bartender made his way back to the table. He reached for Lisa's glass of lingering ice cubes. "Another?" She nodded. "Anything for you, sir?" he said to her dad, but the glass was only half empty.

After letting it sit for a while, Lisa killed the silence. "The blackberries?"

The National Guard had been sent in and the news had been escalating. The blackberries were the darlings of the media terror spotlight: botanical hydras—if one severed a thorny limb, two grew in its place.

"I could use a change of pace," he said.

*

He sold the house, she quit her job. They put an ad in the paper, listing an estate sale, and people came with cash in hand to load furniture into the back of their pickup trucks. "Did anyone die on that chair?" a curious child, about twelve, asked as his mother dug through her purse for the asking price and Lisa shook her head no with tears in her eyes. "I'm sorry," his mother said, quickly extending her hand with the bundle of cash.

Nobody asked if her mother had died on the bed, but she had; she had gotten up in the middle of the night and gone to the restroom. When she came back she told her husband that he was taking over her side of the bed. In the morning she was dead. Lisa's father had told her the story that morning. It was the only time outside of a funeral home she had seen her father cry. Then he'd gone to the bathroom, cleaned himself up and they'd finished with preparations. Some people offered their condolences, but it was hard to accept a stranger's sympathy when they haggled over the price of a mahogany coffee table.

Lisa only saw her brother for a few hours; he didn't make it down until after the estate sale ended. They sat on the ledge of a bay window, picked at the mostly eaten pizza and drank beer.

"How are you holding up?" he said, putting his hand on her shoulder.

"I don't know."

"You don't have to go," he said, and Lisa thought that he sounded sad for her, sincere. How close had they ever been? She wondered if this was a moment they would always look back on.

"Stay here?" Lisa swept her arm across the emptiness of the room. "No, I want to go." In the pittance of light, the dust motes swirling in the air intensified the emptiness. "I wonder if the blackberry bushes have killed, if that's why dad wants to go."

"Jesus Christ," her brother said and got up. He walked a tight circle around the room.

She had forgotten that he was only twenty-one. Despite how he towered over her with elements of that same quiet presence their father possessed, he was still so young, still seven years younger. She felt guilty about letting her sorrow fall onto him. "I'm sorry," she said, "I'm sorry."

He put his arms around her and they cried together because that was what they knew they were supposed to do.

*

The new house in Federal Way, Washington had been built in 1958. It had four bedrooms, two bathrooms and a massive garage. It cost almost half of what their two bedroom in North Carolina had. The owner of the house seethed as he signed the papers, taking deep breaths as he put ink to sheet. "Two years ago," Lisa overheard him say to his realtor as they left the office, "I was offered five times that much. What the hell am I going to do now?"

They furnished the house in Ikea, driving out to South Renton a week before the store was to close. The farther north they went, the more the blackberries were taking over, snaking across roads and overwhelming the forests that crept alongside I-5.

Lisa couldn't remember the last time she'd had a real conversation with her father. When she had come home on weekends, before—before everything—she spent her time with her mother. Dad was always in the garage, tinkering, or he would be in his study, finishing up some work. He'd been an accountant, but retired when her mother died. At the funeral, Lisa held his hand, but they didn't speak. Maybe this was her chance to talk.

"Do you miss Mom?"

He seemed taken off guard by the question. He took his eyes off the road to look at her. They sparkled with moisture. He looked forward again. "Yes," he said, "very much."

"Me too." Lisa said and felt a fool.

When they arrived at the Ikea, there was a huge banner across the front that read: *TOM ROBBINS WAS RIGHT GOING OUT OF BUSINESS SALE*. A picture of a blackberry vine thrusting through the concrete of a sidewalk was vividly rendered in the background. The Ikea building was the only one occupied, the other businesses already gone. The empty buildings like ghosts waiting on a dying friend.

While outside the trees and the berries flourished, the warehouse was skeletal. Like a halfway deconstructed zeppelin, girders stretched from one side of the building to the other, crisscrossing and meeting with support beams. Duct stood starkly against the empty roof and beneath it all was leftover shelving, almost equally barren; their choices were made by scarcity.

"Moving in?" the store manager asked as he rang them up. He told them how his employees had either quit for what little work there was left, or had fled the area entirely, moving out to Walla Walla, Washington; Portland, Oregon or Vineland, California where there were still evergreens and rhododendrons and morel mushrooms without the impossible blackberry bushes. "Welcome," he said in conclusion with a sad smile. He finished their order and handed them their receipt on top of a paperback book with a pack of cigarettes and a woodpecker on its cover. He smiled a wan smile at their confusion and wished them luck.

Lisa dreamt of being smothered in her sleep, of waking to a sea of green spikes before she perished. She didn't share her dreams with her father, though; they didn't speak much, and she wasn't going start examining her nihilistic subconscious with him as their only dialogue.

Weeks were spent in relative tranquility. Her father touched up the house, spending days in the garage, sanding and routing and drilling. Lisa read and sketched. Sometimes her father came out and pulled at the blackberry bushes, sorting through the bramble, gathering up vines and twisting them together, banding them with garbage ties until he cleared out a small patch of the yard.

Lisa's father bought an F-350 from a man who'd refused to evacuate for St. Helens in the eighties. If a volcano couldn't move him, he'd be damned if some shrubs did. Lisa and her father sometimes spent their days driving around downtown Seattle to have a look. They passed National Guard units, armed with flamethrowers and leather gloves and shears, driving Bobcats and backhoes, trying to take the blackberries head on.

"Idiots," Lisa said every time they drove past the cordoned areas. New plants were already growing where vines had been ripped out but the roots remained, or from the smoldering ashes where a flamethrower's chemical fire had burned.

"They'll be gone soon enough," her father said, and by May he was mostly right. Congress grew tired of the money spent and began withdrawing the Guard slowly, avoiding the attention of an abrupt exit. The fire and the shears and the machinery had done nothing, had possibly spurred growth, and the cost was too much.

By the time Lisa and her dad reached the center of the city, they were driving on a green road of blackberry vines that twined tightly together, carpeting everything. Creepers climbed through open windows into apartment buildings and scaled the Space Needle. Eco King Kong. Lisa began to wonder if it had been a good idea to follow her father out West. At first she enjoyed the trips to Seattle. They made her feel empty.

"What are you thinking?" she asked.

"Oh," he said, "just getting ideas."

*

The nut jobs proclaimed the blackberry bushes as justice imposed upon the world. It was punishment for using pesticides, for genetically modifying tomatoes and using hormones on cows. It was because of global warming, because of the exponential increase in greenhouse gasses. It was because people ate meat and wore fur. It was because of the lumber industry. It was because people were sinful:

were gay, had premarital sex, didn't pray enough. It was aliens. It was god. It was our doom. It was the beginning of the Earth's salvation.

*

Lisa's brother flew in after his junior-year finals in May. She and her father again drove up the I-5 to pick him up, the farther north they drove, the more the blackberries choked out everything. There was a red house off of the highway, barely visible. It was covered so thickly it looked like the blackberry bushes were bleeding bits of house.

The airport was a battlefield where the National Guard still had a highly visible presence. Planes flew low over the tops of trees while soldiers pushed and cut and fought the blackberries. The bushes mounted on the edges of the tarmac and waited. When Lisa welcomed her brother with a hug, he wondered aloud if he hadn't been dropped off in the Balkans by mistake.

They grilled on the back patio and enjoyed the evening air, Mount Rainier majestic in the background. The food was good and the view was wonderful.

"I have an idea." Lisa's father told them after dinner. "I'll need both of you."

"Jesus dad, I just got back from school," her brother said.

"I'm going to need both of you." Her brother and her dad locked eyes, but her brother didn't say anything.

He laid it out simply: The mutated blackberry bushes grew in vines rather than bush clumps. They could gather up the vines and weave them together, binding them with copper bands or anything strong enough to hold the mass.

"You're kidding," her brother said.

Lisa looked at the vines gathered up already. There was a clear yard, even if the grass was dead from months of light deprivation. It occurred to her that they should have been doing something a long time before then.

"We start tomorrow," he said, standing. He put his hand on his son's shoulder before he left. "It's good to have you home. Get some sleep."

Lisa suggested hot chocolate and was surprised her brother accepted. He told her about his junior year of college, about criminology classes, which really meant chemistry and psychology and sociology. He told her about the parties he went to and the girls he met. Lisa listened inattentively, thinking about the blackberries.

He grabbed her attention with a grave look. "I ran into Mary Hollins," he said. "At a bar with some buddies. She asked how you were. You should call her."

Lisa was caught off guard by the thought of her childhood friend, but it seemed more like the memories of past life regression. "I don't know," she said, "I'm waiting for something."

"What?"

As she lay in her bed, Lisa pulled up the images of her life before, when she had a mother and hope: friends and drinks and work. Even though she was awake, she dreamed that those memories were drowning in blackberry vines.

*

They went to work. Lisa helped with the thorny vines at first, but didn't last long. She had no aptitude for the separating and twisting and bracing of the blackberries. Her father and her brother seemed born to it though, and the yard was soon transformed. Lisa took artistic control, noting where the bushes were rooted and sketching ideas—soon they had two massive arches on each side of their house, reaching from the front yard to the back and touching the edges of the roof. They strung blackberry vine cables, connecting the arches, and let down thin braids of vine streamers down the sides. They wrapped their work in blue and red string and banded it with aluminum. They arranged the masses of blackberries in the yard into hedges and formed geometrically shaped bushes from stray brambles.

The house converted, they tinkered and relaxed. Lisa envisioned the blackberries in massive towers with cascading tresses of thorny vines. She drew arches with gradually flaring green bases. She imagined the blackberries as vipers that her father and brother had wrangled into submission and drew upon lingering images from mythology. She drew a massive avatar with defined muscles clutching at blackberry vines, dominant. She wrote: Heracles Botanical Design.

They used their house and yard as a portfolio and pitched their company to city officials. "Welcome to our home," Lisa said when the city planners arrived in their faded suits. "This project took us about a week." They showed photographs from before and answered questions of logistics, structures and contracts. They were hired on the spot. They went out for Thai food to celebrate, their mouths a joyous burning, and began work the next day.

They worked well as a trio, Lisa scouting the layout of the streets and the bushes and drawing up ideas. She had a knack for sorting through the ruins of a yard and giving it a future. Her brother and her father exceled in putting plan to action. Lisa stopped dreaming of being smothered by vines, but what filled the void she couldn't say.

After the long days of work, tired and sweaty and covered in scratches from the thorns, they came home and relaxed. On sunny days, they grilled. Lisa watched her brother and father throw a baseball back and forth in wordless motion. The sound of the birds and of the baseball in the soft pocket of leather surrounded her.

What did they think about? Did they need to think about the monotonous motion of throwing? Did throwing and catching require thought or was it instinct? Did they wonder what their life would be if they had stayed back east? Did they think about the blackberry bushes that could be cajoled, but not killed, or the life they had made out west? Did they still mourn in those moments their loss of mother and wife? Or did they think only of the sound a glove makes when they reached their hands into the pocket, the tips of their fingers gripping the stitches and the backs of them softly rubbing against the smooth, oily inside of the glove?

Lisa asked her brother one day what he thought about when he was throwing the ball back and forth.

"I don't know," he said, picking up a glass of water that Lisa had poured for herself. "It's nice."

"But what do you think about?"

"Nothing."

"Nothing?" Even when she wasn't thinking of anything, Lisa found that she was still rushing about, worrying about something, planning for something, wondering about something.

"I just throw the ball and don't think of anything. I guess it's like Zen, or whatever."

"Do you even know what 'Zen, or whatever,' is?" Lisa asked in exasperation.

"It's like throwing a baseball around for an hour."

*

By early August, King 5 news had taken notice of the work being done in Federal Way. They came out to talk to the family. Within a week, a slew of cut-rate imitators had sprung up, underbidding for inferior work. The competitors lacked understanding and artistry, but, the mayor explained, almost sounding apologetic, it was local government, after all.

"I worked so hard," her father said, after the city had pulled the contract with a gaggle of lawyers and some slippery manipulations of loopholes. "Now I have nothing. Now I have nothing again."

Lisa didn't have the words and looked to her brother for support, but he had stormed out of the room. Her mother would have been good at this, she could have pointed out to the family how much good that they'd done, but she was gone, and so the loss of their business felt like death. Another. She put her hand on her father's and they sat there together a long time.

Lisa dreamt that night that she was fighting the blackberries in hand to hand combat, winning easily. Then, behind her, her house blew up. The explosion was purple and gold, the flames the shapes of wolves.

The next day the phone rang early. A homeowner in Bellevue wanted to hire them. She was a widow from an old-money family and wanted the craftsmanship she had seen on the news. Lisa named an overlarge number, purely out of spite for their recent loss, and the woman accepted.

Stunned, Lisa passed the news to her father, who was in his garage, sitting at an empty workbench. The phone rang again, this time a young couple holding out in Kirkland. Again, from Mercer Island. Again, from Sammamish.

The shift to private contracts, to artistry and perfection of craft rather than speed of completion, changed things. Lisa's father insisted on taking as much work on as possible. "You never know how long it will last. Not with this. Not with anything." She knew he was right somehow and that he was wrong. She couldn't thread the ideas, however, she couldn't place their roots. What is the difference between making use and milking dry?

They started work early, before their employers would be up to interfere, arriving at the houses as day broke, wringing what they could of the summer, working until dusk began to settle. Then they drove home in silence, exhausted.

They worked Saturdays. Her brother took a leave of absence from school. They worked through August and September. Sundays were spent in a daze, sleeping until two in the afternoon and going to bed again at nine. They worked almost exclusively along the Puget Sound, rescuing mansions from obscurity, sprucing up the architecture with green. Lisa stopped reading books on a lawn chair in the back yard; her brother and her father stopped throwing the baseball back and forth. They hired extra hands to help disentangle the bramble so that they could thread it more quickly into increasingly complex patterns.

They spun such finery from the brutal vines that a homeowner once joked that soon the rich would begin foolishly importing the blackberries to New England.

Under a cloud of despair, their work leapt from craft to art. A project they finished was the poster child for the "New Architecture." Lisa hoped that the coming winter would kill the blackberries, that they would dry up and shrivel and their leaves would turn yellow like normal blackberries. She knew better.

*

Time dissolved like sugar in coffee, disintegrated and disappeared into the opacity of history. Lisa thought about quitting and moving back to North Carolina, but it was only a sad fantasy. Her work was in Seattle, her new life. What was left in Greensboro she wouldn't recognize.

Even with January snow, the blackberries didn't stop growing. They grew as fast as grief, the vines glistened and reflected the light of the sun, but the beauty was lost on Lisa. She felt like she was rusting when she stood outside in her jumpsuit, trying to hold a pencil through her mittens to sketch designs. One of the workers almost fell off the roof securing an arch to the corner of a house in Medina. Her father caught a cold that spiraled into pneumonia.

"I like being a foreman," he said when she tried to make him take time out to rest. "We move the earth, reshape it. I'm not going to sit in bed just because of a cold. Without this, we have nothing." Even though his nose was running and his eyes were underscored by dark bags and his voice was hoarse, she nodded her head and smiled. Much later, she would wish that she had said they had each other, but it hadn't occurred to her.

A few days later he collapsed.

Lisa and Ben rode with their father to the hospital and sat by his bed. "Don't go," Lisa said. "Don't die. I don't want to be your artist; I want to be your daughter. I want to talk about mom with you. I want to talk about you." They watched the slow traffic of IV medication that did no good. They held his hands until they grew cold.

They had run the routine before: arrangements were made. Time moved forward. "I don't know what I'm going to do," Lisa told her brother when the last of the mourners had left.

"I think it would be best if I went back to school," he said.

"What the hell happened?" Lisa said, but her brother didn't have an answer.

*

They sold the company. They sold the house for seven times what their father had paid for it. When her brother went back to North Carolina for spring semester, Lisa drove to Eureka, California, to find something, she said; she didn't know what. "I'll exclaim if I do." On her way to the airport she noticed that Federal Way was worse for the wear from sloppy work and entropy. Vines once bound tight strayed away, polluting the landscape with their tendrils. As she looked at the sprawl of the old work undone and the wild explosion of new growth, she wondered how long it had been going on right where they lived. She took a taxi to the airport and looked out of the window for the red house along the side of the freeway but there was nothing to see but green.

A month passed in California. The news was how the blackberries were spreading across the country. She tried to call her brother, but he was busy with school, trying to move on with life.

Lisa paced around her apartment until she gave up and finally called Mary Hollins. The friendship that had mattered so much to her in her youth had become a memory best remembered through photographs. The conversation was short and sterile. There was only the exchange of information, the promise to keep in touch, the abrupt silence when the call was ended.

Lisa turned on the television and flipped the channels absently. She thought of a bar but the imposed camaraderie of people gathered together turned her off. A public access show was running a static camera from the space needle, its lens already mostly covered in growth. Lisa settled on the couch, watching the thin grey slice of Pacific Northwest cloud-cover on the screen between the twists of thorns, waiting to see if a final tendril would cut off that last vestige of light or if the sky would remain, dark and cloudy, but there.

Goat Sucker

It wasn't fleeing, it was a roadtrip. It was a chance to bond, an opportunity too rare to pass up and I was blitzed with the possibilities that lay before us; a grown, jobless man and his retired father on the way south in late spring. It seemed good, it seemed right.

It is difficult, of course, to pin down what I had hoped would happen on the trip. I needed to understand my father after so many years of never even trying; there was something screaming that now was the very last time to do so, that if I let this opportunity go I would be marooned, left forever. By showing an interest in the old man now, there could maybe be the kind of reconciliation that afternoon television was made for, something all the more difficult to attain due to the fact that there was no single rift or place of tearing. What separated my father and I was more akin to miscommunication and the simple geography of distance. That we could heal that rift through a road trip seemed symbolic. The geographical distance between myself and the Madison police didn't hurt much either after the obviously ridiculous incident with Speedy Cash.

My latest employment in that long string had been terminated over the matter of my till and the whereabouts of thirty stupid dollars. All I can say about that is that I'm not dumb enough to try and steal from a check cashing establishment, and even if I was, I find it hard to believe that anyone, really, could be so foolhardy as to do it from their own register—talk about asking to get caught. I don't know what happened to that money, an explanation not good enough for my former manager—who was just as unmoved by my suspicions about the shift supervisor— and most certainly found lacking by the interested persons in the eleventh precinct. No one seemed to understand, no matter how much I explained it to them, that I was simply not the kind of person who would be caught doing something so dumb. They all wore the self-righteous smirk of habitual disbelief.

Compounding matters some was the freak accident disappearance of the money order I had taken out to cover my rent that had gotten two months past due. My landlord didn't appreciate the disappearance, but he was kind enough to accompany me to Ace Cash, even though I really had to get my groceries into the fridge before they expired. When I showed them my receipt the lady at the counter said that the check had been cashed already, which was impossible because I had made it out to my landlord, who was standing right there with me and who didn't have his money. I demanded right there that she return the full amount of money as was made out on that receipt, money owed to my landlord, and said I wasn't going to move until we got it. I demanded to see a manager. She called the police instead, like I was trying to pull something on her, but I just wanted to pay rent. I thought about waiting for the cops, because then I could file a claim saying that someone had stolen that money order and cashed it, but of course I knew that would be a dead end, what with the terrible inefficiency of the Madison police department. They would rather persecute an innocent like me than spend the time bothering to catch the real culprit.

In hindsight, leaving said location at a sprint was possibly not the wisest response to the situation.

Matters like that do not make bonding easy, but I was there at least, with my dad, and that was really something. Who cared that I had come to my father in a state of mild, temporary desperation? I could have squatted in his empty house, like he had suggested when I told him I needed a place to crash for while, you know, as things had been going pretty rough for no real reason lately. But when I looked around that sparsely furnished house on Rushmore Lane, with the wild, dead or dying jumble of grass in the back yard, and the dearth of consumer electronics within, aside from the laptop he was bringing with him, staying seemed silly. I realized I didn't just need a new base of operations, so to speak, I needed to connect with my father. Somewhere in the past something had come undone between us, and since I was temporarily free from the constraints of the daily grind, I had the chance to fix it. If I'm being one hundred percent, I suppose that the thought of answering my dad's door one Tuesday morning, or whatever, and facing a load of B.S. questions from detective soandso about the Speedy Cash business, or some old so-called friends looking for something I wouldn't even know about might have been a motivator, but I would like to believe, and in my heart I truly know, that now was the time to get to know my dad and his strange ways.

I didn't have much of an opportunity to tell dad about my plan on the road, but that seemed fine. We drove straight through to New Mexico in just over a day and I developed a headache along with a worrying tickle that I knew could be cured with over-the-counter cough syrup, plenty of water and probably a few ibuprofen.

Since mom died, dad had been stuck in a cycle of fascination, obsession and then boredom with a rotating gaggle of unorthodox beliefs. At first it had been the séances, which was actually sort of sweet. He and mom had gotten hitched right out of high school, one of those sweetheart romances, and that lasted thirty four years before the stroke shuffled her off the refrigerated coil of that Wisconsin winter. Shakespeare via Madison— dad hadn't appreciated that small joke back then. It made sense, anyways, that he'd try to get in touch with her in the afterlife, especially since I was in my own world of grief and personal interests, things that ate into my free time so that I couldn't be there for him like I maybe should have. It was me and mom who ever even fought, not dad, he wasn't the one who had kicked me out of the house when that one thing happened in high school, and yet I skipped her funeral like it was punishing her and not him. Sometimes I look back and think of how foolish I used to be.

The séances didn't work, of course, and dad eventually gave it up, dispirited, and moved on. Instead of coming back to reality though, he went from one crazy idea to the next. He was into voodoo and ghosts, qi energy and breatharianism, crystals and aliens and Native American mythology. Bigfoot only barely escaped his scrutiny. It wasn't just an interest, even if it began casually, it was quickly a full-fledged obsession until dad was so immersed that when he couldn't find the results he was after he had no recourse but to reject the idea wholesale, moping about the house in a near catatonic depression until the next idea, the next great hope came along.

Which is what brought us down to New Mexico in the first place, in search of the Chupacabra. The problem was that there weren't any real sightings in the state. Sure, there were sightings, but even as far as monsters in the dark go, they were ephemeral; the same sort of imagined fancy as my former manager turning the matter of thirty freaking dollars over to the police, like it was a real crime or something. He said that there had been some question over other registers in the past weeks and that with mine coming up short it led him to believe that it was a systemic thing that had its radius squarely centered on my noggin. He must have been born of the same stock as those morons on the internet posting about a reptile-like creature lurking outside of Ruidoso. Any real hard look would prove to anyone of even moderate intelligence that what was happening was the misfiring of some delusional, overstimulated mind seeking an elaborate answer to something pretty straight forward. Me and dad eventually decided that there was nothing to see, and so we loaded ourselves into the truck, headed to more likely places of interest, a technique the Madison PD could take a lesson from. We went to Texas, they should have gone to that slimy looking supervisor.

Before the goatsucker had become dad's latest *raison d'être*, he had been on an extremely long and arduous UFO kick. Things had gotten pretty desperate by then, enough so that his old friends looked me up, eager for someone to make dad shut his yap while at work. It was the kind of crazy, they said, that could annoy someone upstairs enough to get him canned without the compensation his forty years of service deserved and the dumb bastard only had a year left before retirement. I hadn't talked to my father for nearly three years, but even then I knew that he hadn't really been friends with those men since mom died. God, how long had that been? He hadn't really been friends with anyone, actually. Even after all the bridges he had burned with those people with his whackadoodle obsessions, the foundation of friendship had somehow survived. It bothered me, I remember, because my own friends would have sold me down the river for a bump. Talk about predicting the future.

Well, I called the old man up, being in a rare state of clarity after his old buddies had given my cage a good rattle, and he invited me right over. Just like that. So I came on down and we sat in awkward silence in that old living room, not talking about mom or the years or the times. When I broached the topic of his UFOs, he leapt at the opportunity and led me on a tour of his study, eager to regale me with the details of his unsightly passion.

I would guess it began like everything else, with an honest, simple interest. Right before we had fallen out of touch he'd given me a call and an encouragement to install S.E.T.I. at home. I didn't have a computer then, but he'd told me about the theories of alien contact anyway. I'd ignored him out of apathy and because I had my own obsessions, which was why we drifted apart in the first place. Plus, he'd always played the good cop to mom's bad, and without her the dynamic felt wrong. It wasn't until I came over, though, for that tour of the study that I realized things had spiraled out of control. He regaled me with his ideas on crop circles, which I was in no real condition to make coherent, having taken something for my nerves before stopping by to see him that day. He told me about which ones were fake and which weren't; how even though most crop circles were obviously hoaxes and others were simply less obvious ones, there had to be the real deal out there, especially when they first began to appear in anonymous farmers' fields—what were they, he wondered out loud to me, what were they trying to say? You had to look at them as signs, he told me, an obvious olive branch of communication, even if incoherent.

Worse was the group he'd gotten involved with. They were searching for proof of contact; they believed that aliens were on Earth already, in one capacity or another, and it was their, the group's, job to establish a means of communication. The depths of self-delusion were so deep I felt like they must have looped into infinity and I didn't like the abyss in which I stared. I made excuses and got out of there, making sure, in a stroke of lucidity, to eke out a promise from dad that he would calm things down at work so he could remain gainfully employed. That was something, as it came at the cost of me promising to stop by more often. I didn't hold up my end of the bargain, but since he wasn't fired, I assume dad had held up his.

Dad kept asking if I was alright, because I would drift off on the long stretches of road, going somewhere in my head, he'd say, or else passing out and drooling all over myself. I was fine, just fighting that flu, you know?

The whole Chupacabra fix was just an offshoot of all that alien business. I heard about it all on that interminable drive from far north to deep south, and it was bad enough when we were alone. Worse was that he used that same overknowledgeable banter, the kind that could easily secure a seventy two hour involuntary, with every farmer and outskirts drifter he could get to hear him. It surprised me how many people listened, how many were willing to spin their own yarns for him. There was nothing in the great wasteland of New Mexico, as far as dad could figure—to which I supplied a necessary guffaw of obvious statement—but the people certainly had their stories, nearly all of them contradictory and illusory. When dad'd had enough of their imaginations run wild with hope and myth and the occasional outright fabrication—which dad could stand less than anything else, I should know—we skedaddled out east.

Here was the point that confused me. Despite the absurdity of the idea in and of itself, and despite the degree of his obsession, dad never really went over, not fully at least, to the dark side of credulity, holding on like a lunatic with his blankie to the fringe of understanding and reality. Despite the money he'd sunk into his explorations for alien life, among all the others, despite the time and dedication, he never really fell for the snakeoil or hopeful fantasies. His UFO group probably interviewed hundreds of people who claimed to be aliens or in contact or able to get in contact with them, but they were all dismissed, sadly, as crackpots or over credulous. Dad would have made a great cop, superior to the North's current breed. Their crowning moment was going to be a young man who'd claimed to be in contact with extraterrestrials through unnatural vibrations in his teeth. They investigated and found out it was only that the man was, for reasons understood by only electrical engineers and adherents to late night b-movies, picking up the signal for a local Spanish language radio station through his fillings. Poor kid. I guess dad learned pretty well from my teenage years how to decipher the truth from what he wanted to believe, even when the proof came from the deluded mouth of a still-believer.

I remember coming to dad a few months after I'd been evicted, my reserves of cash burned through in ill-advised ways, seeing that look. It was a little like what he'd give to the farmers with their Mexican Monster stories that had an eye towards fooling the simple. Except that there was something different in Madison then, something that had to do with me in particular that I still can't quite figure.

It was this unforeseeable skepticism that always killed his grand ideas. The hopes got bigger and more unwieldy until there came a point where rational thought had to admit that the ground was not going to shake and the earth was not going to open up to reveal some profound mystery of being. Dad would know in those moments that he'd been deluding himself, trying to believe in something he wanted too desperately.

As we crossed the border and left behind New Mexico, I breathed a sigh of relief, glad to be rid of its Martian landscape and limitless heat. With a knowing smile and a wink, however, dad let it be known that we were out of the frying pan and into Texas, so I better calm my jubilant exhalations a bit. We moved into the armpit of the state and it grew muggier and hotter, the AC in the decrepit

Dakota struggling to keep pace with the sun.

By the time we rolled into Granbury, TX, Wisconsin a mere *tres días* ancient history, I was in a pretty bad state, buying up Nyquil D two bottles at a time whenever I could find it. I'd been trying to keep my deteriorating health from dad because I figured it would screw up our bonding if he were worried about me. He'd noticed right away, though, which I had forgotten about, and there was the sweating and the abundant stops in gas station restrooms. Dad said he was pretty concerned, but I told him there was no need to worry. I wouldn't slow him down, the Nyquil was helping lots and I didn't really have a fever, per se, so much as I was just sensitive to the heat. You couldn't blame me for not liking the heat, and it was so goddamned hot.

I soon discovered that the Chupacabra of Texas was a different beast entirely. After we had passed through Coleman and Blanco and into the outskirts of San Antonio, the beast was just an ugly sort of dog, not the lizard of South American legend we'd chased before, with an unusual method of killing cattle. Dad really locked onto this. It wasn't what he wanted, but it had a ring of truth, the feeling of something real. We talked to farmers who'd shot their share of wild animals and to them the Chupacabra was not some alien looking creature with big black eyes. No, they'd had enough of black-eyed aliens if you know what I mean, they would say and I would keep my damn mouth shut. Their Chupacabras turned out, upon expert inspection, to be a coyote with a vicious case of mange or malformed raccoons. A few of the supposedly mythical creatures that had been preserved in giant walk-in freezers were merely xolos. Dad let me know how unbelievable it was to him that this close to the border people didn't know a simple Mexican hairless dog, how they should understand what was right there in their faces, but that only got me to wondering about just how much dad himself knew.

Driving out to Cuero I took a turn for the worse and was on so much Nyquil to keep my symptoms at bay that I became a little worried I would get addicted to the stuff. Dad told me that he needed to take me to a hospital but I told him no. I didn't have the money to pay for those kinds of insurance bills. I had lost that safety net when I had lost my job. I toyed with the idea of going in and giving my ex-boss' name and social security number on the hospital forms, though I couldn't tell you why I had that memorized, because it was his fault in the first place that I was in this situation. In the end I figured it best not to get the police in Texas interested in me as well. I was probably through the worst, anyways, so I told dad he didn't really need to worry. Sure, I had dropped a few pounds since we set off on our roadtrip, but I had finally put things behind me and was beginning a brand new life where me and my dad were united, and those pounds needed dropping anyways.

I didn't much like the new Chupacabra. It was too ordinary, too mundane. It wasn't that it was becoming plausible that bothered me, but that this seemingly plausible explanation was linked to such extraordinary circumstances. Even though it was just a derivative of a dog, there were still the three holed exsanguinations. The nod to reality made the whole situation even more farcical. Dad just shrugged, like maybe he was on the way down from this particular obsession and told me that everyone has some myth, some legend that they choose to believe.

That the particulars get changed doesn't seem to matter much, what was important was understanding something difficult to comprehend and these people were doing the best that they could. I guess I agreed with him, but I still didn't like it. I wished people would simply call a duck a duck or in this case a monster a monster or else a satanic cult or a couple of kids with a box of syringes and too much time on their hands. Dad grunted his agreement and I knew that our bridge had at least a foundation, if not the arch and span I envisioned.

It was the same story in Cuero, only the weather was even worse, the southeastern section of Texas being the swampass of the United States, I decided, though I had never been to Louisiana, so I might have been wrong. I don't know. Like everywhere, dad grabbed his doodads and whatsits, grabbed baggies for samples of whoknowswhat and took notes with his pad and pen. I started feeling a little afraid by then, both because I felt like my guts were being liquefied and because I didn't want the trip to end. There was still some barrier between me and dad that I needed to eliminate, but I still couldn't exactly place it. I needed more time. Home seemed a worse and worse place to go, not only because I had no apartment or job or that I'd exhausted all my friends and favors. It wasn't just that the Ace Cash problems had snowballed into the Speedy Cash ordeal or that this had morphed into some sort of larger casefile that included other former places of my employment and my various check cashing habits—I didn't even get the money from Ace, so what was the problem? The real, honest to god, swear upon my life reason was that this proximity with dad was going to be gone, he was my traveling buddy and my confidant and we were connecting in ways before unimaginable. Sure, I was sick now, but I would get better. I was probably getting better already.

The last farmer we talked to was a conman through and through who tried to sell us a story so patently bogus my eyes rolled into my head of their own volition, like an animal afraid of bullshit. I happen to have been a person, in my old life, who needed to stretch the truth a bit to get by and so I knew the difference between the semi believable and the outright chainyankers, and this was off the charts. Dad kept taking his little notes though; he was even suckered into buying a few pieces of the crap that man was hocking, so-called genuine shards of nail from the Chupacabra. I confronted dad, even though I felt like my eyes were falling out of my head, and told him I couldn't believe that he had swallowed such an obvious line. He told me that sometimes stories didn't add up, but that didn't mean that the intention wasn't there. He told me that mountain gorillas were considered a myth for hundreds of years, and it wasn't until 1902, when one was shot and killed by a European, that the tales of the so-called savages were finally taken seriously. There'd been too many disparities in the stories, sure, fact mixed in with frightened exaggeration perhaps, but it had been true all along. There was, he told me, the pearl to be found in the mud, but only if you looked. It was hard work looking at dirt and shit all day, but it could be worth it. I told him the money would have been better spent, maybe for some medicine for his son, for example. I told him that when he knew a line was bogus he should nip it in the bud, because if you didn't stop chasing lies, you would spend your whole life staring at nothing but shit and then where were you?

Later that night, at the hotel, dad told me that he wouldn't be heading home yet, which was fine with me until he told me he was going on into Mexico and he might keep going south after that. I didn't have a passport and besides I didn't need the hassle of trying to get myself through official checkpoints, sometimes things didn't necessarily stay localized, though I just told dad about the passport. He shrugged like always and gave me a thousand dollars stuffed in a white envelope he had pulled from absolutely nowhere, and told me it should be enough for what I needed, and a flight home. He said I should probably go to a doctor, have them take care of my flu, or whatever, when I got there. He said he would be back in maybe a month. He wanted to hear the stories of the lizard Chupacabra, he wanted the tales of the Central American alien, the raw and horrible thing that made people afraid to leave their house, even if his Spanish was of the high school yooper variety, and he hoped to see me when he got back.

I was walking in the dark for my medicine when I saw it. It wasn't more than twenty feet away, slinking out of the tree line. It was the eyes that gave it away, the eyes that changed everything, that shone like the world was ending. Like it knew. I stood there until it slunk back from where it had emerged, the twenty in my hand gone sweaty and crumpled, and I thought, dad, you are not going to believe this, but I have to tell you something.

When We Become Two Creatures

Jeff said that it wasn't normal. That most families don't have a box they enter for an hour or more at a time, standing silent and motionless and emerging with their body covered in bruises. Lynn tried to see things from his point of view, but what did Jeff know about normal? It was what her family did.

Lynn was forced to admit at such times that as great as he was, in a lot of meaningful ways, Jeff was a little closed-minded. He tried though. Like when he saw his first in-person gay couple, and the two men kissed, Jeff twitched. But Lynn could see that inside of him there was a battle going on, where what he had been raised to believe and what he had come to understand were in dialogue. He was trying. That mattered. Ignorance was only the lack of knowledge, and can be fixed through education. Experience. So when Jeff said that the box wasn't normal, Lynn didn't say anything. She just patted his hand, like he was a dear child and told him she had to get ready for work.

It came up again a week later. Lynn emerged from her box with the contentment of a postcoital shower. Her arms and legs looked like she had only-just survived a medieval tower's winding staircase. Jeff was on the couch looking worried, telling her that whatever she was doing, it was dangerous.

"It's like aerobics," she told him. "It's like yoga."

By the time she iced and bathed, the blueblack faded into the olive of her skin, and to all but the most investigatory eye, it wasn't even there. "Progress requires sacrifice."

God bless him, Lynn thought, as Jeff screwed up his face to keep from spewing his first thought, turned on his heels, and went out the front door. He's trying.

Later that night, Jeff climbed into bed and lay on his back, his hands behind his head, his arms puffed out like little chicken wings. "People will think I hit you."

"Oh honey," Lynn said. She rolled onto her side and cradled his body in her arms until he released his bird posture, so angry and hard, and softened into her. She felt like there was something else for her to say, something he needed to hear, but she didn't know what it was. Instead, she just held him to her until she felt him go limp.

Jeff took care of himself, preparing his body at the gym, his mind at the office, but he wasn't willing to go further, to develop what was inside him. Lynn's mother used to tell her that there are different types of people, strong in different ways, and she began to think, not for the first time, that maybe, as wonderful as he was, Jeff simply wasn't the person for her.

When Lynn came to her mother with these fears, she received the advice of patience, the gentle shooshing of a mother soothing fears, and then, later, the grudging admission that most men simply aren't strong enough. "It's just biology dear," she said, a bit condescendingly, "don't hold it against him."

A few times, Lynn came home and found Jeff in the box. But he always emerged unscathed, untouched, unmoved. "It doesn't work," he said.

"Oh, darling," Lynn said. She didn't want him to feel slighted, to feel like he was the kid not chosen. But Jeff would shrug off her affection, go to the gym. He would come home still red-faced and see Lynn freshly showered, the bruises still on her, the bloom on her back like dark wings of some unknowable portent. She didn't push it. Maybe she should have. Maybe these moments were possibilities.

As Lynn honed in on her practice, the bruising became more intense, covering her skin entirely, no longer content with just a piece. Jeff waited for Lynn to emerge, increasingly upset. Look what it was doing!

"Don't you remember when you pulled a hamstring," Lynn asked, "and your thigh looked like a hurricane destroying Florida?"

"That isn't the same thing."

"No," Lynn said. "It's a metaphor. It's never the same thing. It is something different, something more."

Jeff had no response.

Then she split. She was in the box for three hours. Her longest. She focused her mind to the part of her that was deeper than biology, and she called to it. It was time. Like an angler, she danced her lure. Like a gymnast, she stretched beyond. The box helped, of course. She summoned that preternatural thing which is the very power, the very self, the essence of being. Oh, when she was able to finally, actually, grasp it! It didn't slip like before, a tease on the fingertips, burning and lingering in her mind for hours after. It was like an action movie, when the hero catches the falling friend, and the clasp is secure, hands and wrists and safety.

When she emerged, Jeff was on the couch, again, waiting, again, fuming, again. Lynn was not bruised this time, or raw, or glowing. Lynn was not alone, either. His features splintered, his face like it didn't remember how expressions would normally fall.

Lynn understood. She packed his things for him, while he sat on the couch, unable to understand. And when she was finished, he just nodded and made his way out of the door.

The world was like it was new. It was comparable to when you had your first kiss: you didn't even know that there was this feeling, that your body was capable of such fragile, tender joy. But this was from inside. Only her, only her. She didn't know what was in store, not yet, surely something great. She showered, the stream of water splitting against her, the world made larger.

Dips

There are some that like to Dip together. My dad for instance. His friends would come over on Friday nights, and they'd all pull out their little boxes and jack into the same memory of when they were in high school, lives peaked at the ripe age of seventeen. Dad had been a quarterback for his little school and he'd thought then that his life was at the ignition stage of an unprecedented rocket, preparing to lift off out of the atmosphere in a long and elegant arc, leaving behind only the smoking trail of greatness. The memory dad and his friends accessed over and over again is the big one, the championship game where he was dodging one lineman and then another as they bulldozed their big bodies just-past him, and right as a linebacker the size of a Smartcar zeroed in on his lithe frame he found the spot between the myriad bodies and across the expanse of the lined grass field, and he sailed the ball thirty-two yards, with unreal accuracy, into the hands of Eric Anderson. This was the play that would turn the tide of the entire game.

When they were done, dad and his friends would all pull

their plugs and slide off their visors and their eyes would open and perform that dumb, blank look while their brains disentangled reality from induced-reality and they could focus again on the drabness of the life that sat before them. They would mutter about the power that my father had then, how marvelous he was, and dad would shake his head and smile, and then, when they were gone, he would sit in his chair and stare at a turned-off television wall and grow darker and darker. Sometimes he'd ask me to bring him the headset again, disappearing into its black plastic and OLED pallor.

This never made sense to me. The memory I always came back to was a shameful one. One I never let anyone see. Never would. It is the proof of my failure as a moral human being. Like anyone, I was imperfect and flawed, but once I had truly fallen. I played it again and again. Each time I felt the pit of my stomach perform its octopus clench, sweat beginning to bead in unhappy anticipation as it prickled with the faint breeze of the evening. And I knew then, again for the first time, that I was not what I had hoped I would be. That I would never be that person, the one who would do the right thing in the right situation when it truly counted. I would always be barely worth the brief glance people gave me before their eyes slipped past, before forgetting I had ever existed. Sometimes I cried after the Dip. Not always. I was always glad to be back to the world, the real one, where I could pretend that I was not that person.

The FTC officially declared that Direct Immersion Playback Systems were a public health hazard. A warning was printed right on the box. Not that it mattered. It wasn't a hardware problem, there were no unethical or monopolistic business practices. The government couldn't actually ban the device, only warn against it. Only put out official statements. Remember how effective that was for cigarettes when they were literally killing users by the millions. Dips was a hazard because it was too good. It was too nice to replay the scenes from the best day of your life, over and over again.

Everyone starts with a few memories. They are harmless and wonderful. Ever wondered what your first birthday was like? All of that joy and preparation and happiness, and you never even knew what was going on around you. Relive it. Your wedding day. Your first love.

Some people branch out. Try to learn. Supplement your flying lesson with a pilot's memory of a near-miss. You do not suddenly become a great pilot, but you can feel the way that they think things through, the way they flip through their checklist, what is internalized and what is instinctual. Or get inside the head of a management guru as they plan for the big meeting. Pick your poison. Hollywood tried to make movies for the Dips, but they couldn't get it to work. Among the other problems, the stuntmen would be thinking about the tricks and gimmicks, the actors would be thinking about marks and lines (except for the psychotic ones, who were so far embedded in the imagined interiority of their character it was a kind of Dips in and of itself).

There was one playback man, Leonard Leonardson (no joke), a kind of human camera, who was able to somehow wipe himself of his own thoughts, experiencing only what he was supposed to at any given time. And so he would watch the stuntmen and think: wow, that is incredible.

He would watch the lovers parting and he would think: wow, that is very sad. He would listen to a joke and he would think: wow, that is quite funny. They made twelve movies with him as observer, the audience as observer—like normal—only they were forced to feel, through Leonardson, exactly how they were supposed to. But then a crazed fan killed him to get at his brain, to make Dips scenes of his whole life. But Leonard Leonardson didn't have a life. It was the disappointment that made the sicko turn himself in. Leonard Leonardson would stand on the movie set and think: wow, this is a movie set. He would wake up and pee and think: wow, I'm urinating.

They tried to make movies with implanted feelings to cover up what the actor or stuntman was actually thinking, those very technical, professional, movie thoughts, so that you would feel like you really were the secret agent, but the gloss on top made it feel like someone was rubbing grape jelly on your occipital lobe. Total bust.

They tried porn, too, but it was also a failure for the most part. Not all that many people wanted to pay good money to think of baseball and unattractive grandmothers or a looming rent payment in order hold out a little longer. Or force themselves to smile despite their leg beginning to cramp while a table dug into their lower back. They didn't want to feel annoyed at the director, or disgusted with their partners. People already got that in real life, they went to porn for the fantasy.

So really, all that was left was what had come first. Dipping into memories. Going back to those moments you wanted to remember. When things were wonderful, or at least when they were actually good. When you were happy.

When mom died, dad doubled down on the memories. But I never saw him remember her. Only those far-away times when he was on top of the world. Maybe he revisited mom, taking in those intimate moments, with the woman he spent more than thirty years with, in a more private location. I only ever saw him with the silly things. Old sports, ancient accomplishments.

Dad slipped further and further with the Dips. Going longer and longer. Some days he would repeat the same memory over and over. When the device wasn't covering his head, he would pace around the house, muttering to himself, chuckling over some phrase or another. "I'll show you a cartographer. I'll show *you* a cartographer."

It was hard to take. This was a man who had been the driving force of getting-it-done, who valued hard work above all, and he was wasting away. Of course, he'd been wasting away for some time, and this was only a last-ditch call to happiness, plugging himself desperately into the past, when he had really been something. Do slackers smoke pot and play videogames because they have nothing to contribute, or do they have nothing to contribute because of it? But I was the pothead with the job, who was doing something with his life, and dad was the hard-driven worker with nothing to do, the badass huddled on the couch, twitching with involuntary muscle spasms, when the dream world accidentally intrudes into the real through micro-muscular synaptic spasms.

I confronted him about it, but he blew me off. "This is what retirement is for. You relax, and enjoy the fruits of your labor." I asked him if heroin was the next step. What better way to relax? He did not take kindly to the question. He told me that I couldn't understand, which was probably true. He told me that I would have had to accomplish something first, which started a fight. I ended up going to my office to get a jumpstart on a merger that would acquire a useful patent. He went to his room to Dip.

I ran a tech company, and so I stayed busy. And so I was the one responsible for his addiction. Dad and I didn't fight that much, but only because I was usually gone, and because I could hire care workers to keep an eye on him. When we actually saw each other, I tried not to pick fights. I tried not to let him pick them with me.

Quanticall was a successful business before anyone at our startup ever realized what a terrible name we had. "It's like quantum mechanics," I told my dad, "because we are making use of science-forward technology, but it's also like a phone call, because we're connecting people." Dad just frowned and said that if I believed that shit, I deserved to have such a dumb name. Point: dad.

When I told dad he shouldn't Dip so often, he said, "What? I can't be proud of the only goddamned thing my son ever did?" The words brought actual tears to my eyes, as he was not a man who often expressed pride, but I was still angry at him. Even the compliment was a fight. Because he was a junkie justifying a fix. Because I was powerless in the face of it.

I told him that if mom could see him now, she would be sick. Sick at what he'd become. A shell of a man. Even as I said it, I was replaying the words in future regret, under a headset.

He hit me. He really was a shell of the man he'd been. He was wasting away, a good third of his size even five years ago, but he was no tech geek, and the punch to my gut flattened me. I doubled and fell, choking for breath. He kicked me in the ribs. He kicked me again in the face. He did this more than once.

When I came to, dad was Dipping in his room. I made an emergency appointment with my doctor but it wasn't that bad. A bit of a concussion, a bruise on the ribs. Things that hurt, but wouldn't hurt me. What was a bruise, in the scheme of things?

Memories change. We knew this before, from all those studies, in labs, and in the criminal justice system. The surer a witness said they were, for instance, the more often they were wrong. Something happens to what you remember. When a piece of our life was re-examined, it would become too-sweet, or too-dark. We had essentialized it, woven it into the tapestry of our narrative: I became like X because Y happened. Think of the person that stole your story and made it theirs, and never even knew they had done it. I imagine I've done it as well. But the trick is, when we do it, we never know. We only find out that something has changed when we see a video of the past, or when we compare memories with someone who has their own version.

I remembered my dad as a Minotaur. A figure of myth, barely glimpsed, barely human. Terrifying. Stories of his feats made up the mass of his substance. He was always "when your father gets home," roaming the maze of the labyrinth, waiting. When I was older, I thought of the tragedy of the Minotaur. A cursed child, the result of some other person's sin, some other person's wrath of judgment, a monster that couldn't be blamed for monstrosity, because monstrosity was given to it. Nana always seemed sweet to me, of course, but we all know that broken bottles become beautiful, turning from razor edges to satin pebbles, when they have been run through the tumble of the sea for decades.

As dad slipped further into his brain, and the caretakers turned into nurses, who warned of further slippage, he fell more often into the dull black of the plastic helmet, the visor over the eyes, the sensors pressed into the pittance of his hair, the flesh of his scalp. He would twitch and smile. I could almost see the arc of the football, taking that precise angle, finding those waiting hands.

I used to Dip regularly. Everyone on the team did. We were breaking new ground, and it was exciting. Plus we had to troubleshoot. Remembering is reliving, and we had to figure out how to induce sleep paralysis to keep the body from running you into a wall or the road. We needed to keep the more prurient remembrances from becoming *too* real.

Like many, probably most, I spent a lot of those first times reliving some favorite sexual encounters. One stood out in particular. A girl just a little too beautiful for my friends to believe, and the sex had been incredible. I came back to it a dozen times in less than a dozen nights. The look of her, the feel of her skin, the rasping of our breathing. It was only after those first dozen times that I could detect the faintest trace of boredom lurking in her eyes. Or disgust. Disbelief. As if the thing that was happening was fine enough, but it was a travesty that it ever should have gotten to this point. The next time I revisited the scene, I could clearly suss out the look of disinterest, in the next I realized that it had been open hostility the entire time. Or maybe that was only my insecurity. Memories change. We change them. I never went back. Perhaps that scene could become something pleasant if I ever came back, perhaps it would turn darker.

I'd met the woman again, maybe a year after the Dips had hit the market. "Do you ever," she said, looking embarrassed and emboldened, and a little horrified, "remember that night?" I told her I did, but that it was too precious to put through a machine. If I remember it right, she had looked relieved.

Sometimes dad would have trouble remembering to eat. Sometimes it was the fault of a mind that had begun the slow unzipping of coherence, but mostly it had to be the hubris of touching the sun. But here, I was Daedalus, creating a thing of such power, and dad was the one who flew too close to those fleeting-and-gone moments of bliss. This much was sure, if you were an ancient Greek, the most likely path of your life was having to solve some riddle or escape some form of imprisonment. Those men and women kept perishing, as I recalled.

Dad's friends came over a few times a week. As often as they could. They would shoot the shit for an hour and then plug in. It wasn't always dad's memory, but it usually was. He was too far gone some days to handle another person's mind. He had grown tenuous as to what was happening and what had happened, and so the complications of another mind, another experience, another person's life could become overwhelming. He would grow belligerent when he took off the headset, he would think we were trying to trick him.

I asked them what it was like, back in the day. What dad was like. At first they capitulated to the memories and the machine.

I pressed them though. "But what was it *like*?"

They thought about it. "It was high school. We were kings, we were popular and successful and liked, but it was high school." They shrugged and left. Never offered to let me share one of those memories of theirs.

I resented having them in my house. They were friends with my dad for my entire life, their history reaching back to the days of middle school, and there was something about them that left a bad taste in my mouth. After high school, they all took dead-end jobs that destroyed their bodies slowly, and they would get off of work, go get drinks, and complain about their kids, their wives, and their jobs. On the weekends, they would sit out in the sun on their lawnchairs "won" by redeeming tickets from cigarette packages, and down beers. They would talk shit and get wasted, yell at the kids to do some menial task or another, and cackle together like crony conspirators.

Dad didn't leave the house much in the first place. The dementia began creeping in right around the time mom died. He could have pushed it off by listening to doctors ("I'm not letting a bunch of eggheaded dipshits dictate my diet and schedule"), but he collapsed into the Dips instead. Heal thyself. Perhaps, in this way, it was a kindness for his friends to come over. They'd been coming over their entire adult lives, but maybe this was something different. I didn't spend enough time with him, not with work, not with the FTC breathing down our neck about addiction. Not with a history I couldn't ever move past. It haunted me. I wasn't a great son, but I had done my part. He wasn't a great dad either.

He forgave me, a little, I suppose. I probably forgave him a little bit too.

I went to my room and put on my own headset. My brain was ready to go. My body knew the ritual. In the machine, my mom told me that I needed to take care of my father. That he needed my help. He was too proud to ask for it, but she wasn't. I was in the hospital, staring at her, as the tubes and the machines made their beeping and wheezing noises, as the doctors and nurses and patient care assistants bustled about in the background.

"Sweetie," she said.

"I can't," I said.

Mom sat up a little, her eyes a little watery. "He loves you," she said. "He's proud. He just doesn't—" She fiddled with the IV taped to the back of her hand. Her skin was papery and sallow. It seemed to glow a faint yellow, like an incandescent bulb with the barest filament. "He needs your help. You have to take care of him."

"I can't." I said. Again. "I can't. Having him around is torture."

"I'm not asking," she said, finally. "This is my last wish. You have to do it."

"The hell I do." I got up, paced the room angrily. "You'll be fine, and you and him can arrange for what needs arranged. I'll give you the money. Just keep him out of my hair. Keep him away from me."

"Sweetie," she said.

"I can't."

"Then you don't love me." With this, she closed her eyes and cried silently.

"Fuck you," I told her. "Fuck you for saying that. Fuck him for everything, and fuck you for this. I'll see you later. I love you mom, but goddamn you for putting this on me."

I almost collided with the nurse as I stormed away, trying to get away from mom's tears.

It was only twenty minutes later when dad called. Mom was dead. She had passed. The first thing he said to me, even though I knew she was dead, because you can tell in the way that the breath catches, the way that the air is letting you know that it isn't moving anymore, that it has stilled, the first thing he said was: "What did you say to her?"

I took off my helmet and wiped my eyes. I regretted the hard words I'd said to her, but I was happy that even in my anger I made sure to tell her I loved her. It was a solace, a small one. I took the deep breaths I needed to calm myself, to bring myself back to normal. I put on the headset again, I clenched my teeth, and I turned it on. I continued the ritual. I prepared myself for my shame, I was ready to experience the memory of my true failure. I pressed play.

The Fuhrer Boys

Once, as a dare to myself, I confessed to the crimes of my employment. It was to Allison, my barista, with whom I was engaged in the slow act of seduction, tricky because she knew my wife of only a few years. I did it because I was horny and because I wanted to prove myself. I wanted to be brave. I never tried it again, I was too afraid of the consequences.

"Come on," Allison had said, "What is it you really do Mr. Government man?"

It would occur to me later that I had never told her before then that I worked for the government. But really, who had the kind of time and disposable income to come into a coffee shop on a daily basis, sometimes twice a day? Who could even get a daily street pass?

"Well," I told her, in my most serious, solemn voice. "You have to swear yourself to silence. I could be killed for leaking this."

Allison leaned in and cooed, so well-practiced I half expected her to take perch on my shoulder. "Killed, huh? You must really trust me."

"I do," I said, and then I explained that I was a supervisor on a government project that had implanted cloned embryos of Adolph Hitler into the wombs of unsuspecting mothers across the country via a conspiracy of IVF clinics. Why would we do this? To better understand the ideas of nature and nurture, of course, to know exactly where upbringing and genetics overlap, where we are trained and where we are destined, so that the United States could better understand, predict, prepare, and control the future leaders of the world.

By the time I finished saying it out loud, even I barely believed it.

She laughed. I laughed.

That story got me laid, insinuating a clever, edgy kind of humor I didn't really have. By the time Allison figured that part out, we'd already built a new life upon the wrecking grounds of my first marriage. It was the only time I ever played my cards so boldly. This was partly from fear, but partly because I lost that insatiable urge of youth to impress and fuck every pretty little thing I laid my eyes upon.

I was not the head of the Seminal In-vitro Evolutionary Genetics experiment, nor did I come up with the idea, but I believed in it. I still do, if not in the same way. My job was to find appropriate families for the embryos, accommodating for complicating factors. We wanted variety, from artistic encouragement to political spectrums. We had to control for levels of nationalism within the family and within the region. We were especially careful when it came to the touchier aspects of the subjects, like race.

I had just finished my postdoctoral work in evolutionary pathopsychology, had just published on the genetic ties that crusade-era military leaders had to Genghis Khan, examining psychological versus genetic predispositions. Apparently, I was exactly what they were looking for. Our country was in a downward spiral towards mediocrity, our only accomplishments being reality celébutants and VR contact lenses (I lost mine one time while walking through a middle class neighborhood and the starkness of the reality made me dizzy with repulsion), so I understood why we were seeking something, or someone, that could lead us into a brighter future.

I was in the midst, back then, of what would become full blown alcoholism, afraid of that seemingly inevitable future. My father was an alcoholic and his father before him, so I had a reason to be worried. I had a reason to put my stock of faith, depleted nearly as much as the Euro, in the outcome of our experiments.

My first marriage would survive a few years, but it was already doomed when I took the job. The time required of me for such a high-level government position didn't help. Partly it was my drinking, mostly it was my devotion to work, but if I ever complained about my marriage to a friend at a bar or a colleague in my workplace, I would boil it down to a single mistake: I had married a woman named Shirley who didn't like Leslie Nielsen.

"I think you've had enough to drink," Shirley would say at, for instance, the neighborhood barbeque, not long after we had moved in.

"Shirley you're joking," I would say, sloshing my arm outwards to draw in the helpless bystanders, a big grin on my face, tight smiles on theirs. They got it.

"No, I think it would be best," Shirley would say, completely oblivious.

"Shir-ley you're joking," I would say, breaking it down for her. Nothing. "Sure-ly?" I tried on the variation, hopeful. "Shi-erly, Sur-ely. Shi-shu, shi-shu. Whatever, it's a quote, damn it."

In hindsight, yes, like so many things that I know now, this was not about Shirley or slapstick comedies, but would it really have killed her to indulge me in that one stupid joke? We didn't attend all that many neighborhood barbeques.

*

The thing about secrecy is that it is a Tribble. Or a Gremlin. Fine if you keep it all alone, you starve it and isolate it. Feed it, though, and it explodes progeny. Keeping a secret doesn't just mean containing the number of people that know about it, it means having a big enough space to warehouse everything—especially when you're talking about national security. So in order to keep the Fuhrer Boys—that's what we took to calling them—secret, we had had to know everything about them. This meant setting up fake fertility clinics, digging up information on the families, the neighborhoods, everything. We created this big, black umbrella of redirects, political deference and disinformation to hide ourselves. And once you have this kind of umbrella, you start seeing just how many things you can fit under it. In our case, wiretapping allowances set up to fight terrorism, and fertility clinic "examinations" to keep illegal clones at bay (illegal being the key, as we had been cleared by the Attorney General herself). But when things get crowded under the formally too-big umbrella, when all those new Gremlins start to push against each other, you find yourself needing more space, so you go and buy yourself a bigger umbrella. We barely had to do anything, just re-interpret a few laws, ask a few favors.

*

I left Shirley, riding the wave of power I felt from fucking a nineteen year old barista and the thrill of reshaping the country's future. She was old news, and I was at the top of my game. Allison, too, was more understanding of my drinking. We had begun our affair at the bars of high-end hotels, the intoxicating effects of liquor cast a spell of excitement almost as potent as my ability to buy it. These were the first years of the GM plague—who thought that granting a monopoly to a single seed producer was a good idea?—when the distillation of alcohol was largely outlawed for all but those at the highest rungs of the bureaucratic ladder.

My team devised a series of tests to track the social progress of the Fuhrer Boys. In one, we planted kids of various ethnicities in a controlled environment, for instance a doctor's waiting room, and studied the interactions between the children. Sometimes the parents would sit there and passively observe, other times, it was the parents themselves who were the test.

Most of the interactions were more subtle, of course, the mere presence of people of foreign color, accent or nationality: a woman in a hijab, an Armenian-looking (we were assured) man in a lightly stained tank top, Canadians saying "aboot." We would plant so-called normals in the lobbies, someone of the same background as the test parents, to sit and provoke a reaction. They might express horror about some bit of news, the Russian involvement in the Bakersfield Portfolio incident that had gutted the middle class, or the inevitable collapse of the Anglo-French tradegroup. We would translate the cries of agreement or the uncomfortable, non-committal nods into points of data that I would later attempt to correlate to the development of the Fuhrer Boys.

One day I had come home and Allison was in the living room, waiting for me. This was about six months after we were married, when things were good. Before I'd had her bugged and followed.

"Hey," Allison said. She met me at the door and planted a kiss that seemed designed to make the worries of work disappear. Even then I was beginning to see that the Fuhrer Boys were not entirely within the realm of my understanding. One of them had set fire to a bunny and invited a collection of friends—of all colors and nationalities—to enjoy its roasted flesh. What the hell was that supposed to mean?

"Hey yourself." I picked her up in my arms and I kissed Allison like her lips were my redemption. She was so young and she made me feel so damned good to have her.

After I put her down, Allison looked up at me; she was very short, five foot nothing, her black hair done in a pixie cut and said: "What's the best thing about fucking twenty one year olds?"

God she made me so horny. I was almost overcome. "I could think of a few."

"There are twenty of them," she said, giggling and standing up on her tippy toes, pushing her lips lasciviously into mine.

I suppose that was a joke in line with impregnating women with Hitlers. She had thought that I was edgy and funny. That's hindsight, though. Then, I didn't understand how sex with an infant could be a joke. Worse was the brutal reminder that she wasn't even twenty-one herself. With her tiny frame and adolescent haircut (along with the cheerleading costume she was fond of seducing me with), she was the perfect legal jailbait, the cowardly pedophile's dream girl. What kind of a future, I thought, is derived from seeking the past?

"I don't like those kinds of jokes." I sat down on the couch, letting myself flop the last few inches. Allison crawled into my lap, oblivious to what was going wrong. She wanted to stir me up, but I was too guilt stricken and old and she was so very young. It didn't happen. Maybe I knew right then how our situation would end. If I did, though, I displayed an aptitude for self-deception.

"Okay," Allison said at last, giving up on what she was doing to my neck, sliding her legs off my thighs and stretching herself out next to me. "You tell me a joke, then."

"Okay," I said. "What word starts with 'N,' and ends with 'R' that you never want to call a black man?"

Allison thought about it for a second. I could tell she was afraid the answer was the obvious one.

"Neighbor," I told her. Oh, how I laughed.

Allison didn't laugh. She got this look on her face that I had seen before, though never so frankly, never for as long as it lingered then. The joke, I know now, is that we were racists who are afraid of being caught by certain words, as if our not being caught was what made us not racist. But only Allison got it at the time.

*

When the Fuhrer Boys were four, despite clear trends, I decided that our data wasn't comprehensive enough. We needed a better control group. We expanded the umbrella to include a random sampling of the population that we would tag and monitor. It made perfect sense, but I had some trepidation about bringing it up. How would the Cabinet feel about spying on innocent Americans? It turns out that they were wildly enthusiastic. The population had grown restless, concerned as it was with silly things like income distribution and governmental control of personal liberty. The riots, the strikes and the protests were really just a form of domestic terrorism, weren't they?

This was when I had Allison bugged, as I mentioned before. I suppose I had checked out of my relationship. I'd started drinking without her, going to different bars and telling her I was working late, much like I'd done to Shirley. Through the natural laws of habitual alcohol consumption, I met women, I had affairs, I repeated myself again and again. Alcohol, meet my friend Ouroboros.

Allison didn't take this lying down. She remembered her own history and wouldn't let me get off so easily. Like the Europeans, she took advantage of every opportunity to move money into her own private accounts, secure assets and then, boom, divorce papers. Sure, it took years, but it still came from nowhere.

This gets away from me. The divorce didn't happen until the Fuhrer Boys were fifteen. Allison didn't start hiring detectives and honeypots until a year before then. It was when the Fuhrer Boys were six—seven years before my second divorce—that it seemed obvious that they were as genetically predisposed to power plays and homicidal tendencies as I was to drink and sex. I was obsessed with stopping it, sure that something could be done.

In the meantime, the world had caught up. The Russians had heard of our scheme and made fifty clones of Stalin to outdo us, the French had eighty Napoleons (crossbred, it must be said, with strains of basketball players for the height necessary in modern politics), the British inconceivably produced a dozen Margaret Thatchers. In a fit of nationalistic fervor we went back to the drawing board with our own clones of national heroes, but none ended up being fit for duty. Our Washingtons turned out too simplistic, our Roosevelts too interested in sci-fi movies for reasons we couldn't quite figure and our Jeffersons were painfully, unanimously, racist.

As for myself, I was cycling between months of sobriety and desolation. Nature seemed to be the biggest deciding factor for the Fuhrer boys. We began working on genetic enhancements to better control their progress. Were we nervous about giving doses of Superman juice to the offspring of a homicidal maniac? Of course we were, but early tests had shown the serum to enhance traits of docility even as it tended to exacerbate charisma. We had to do anything we could.

We manipulated the clones' appeal, their strength, their intelligence, their facial symmetry. We orchestrated shifting economic conditions, we redistricted neighborhoods, manipulated friendships, fostered affairs with teachers; I doubt there was a scenario we didn't think of. One of the Fuhrer Boys was elected to his class presidency by promising to lead an armed mob against their rivals in football, fulfilling his mandate with a melee that local area police had never seen the likes of. Another organized a bike gang. This was when they were ten; by the time they had become teenagers, they were being actively recruited by politicians and Cartel bosses.

And what was my own inevitable repetition of history? It was Lori, my assistant. This isn't to say that she was another young girl not yet aware of what was coming down the road. It wasn't a complete repeat. Lori had her own PhD in Cognitive Dissonance and the night we spent together was more than likely a pity fuck she threw my way.

I was still in charge of my unit, and in fact had just received a commendation from the President for my work. I wasn't proud of it, but sometimes any kind of accolade feels good. The Fuhrer Boys, by that time, were absolutely, positively going to take over the world. The administration (you know which) had decided that given our current economic situation (dire), our current political clout (we had just lost the Olympics to Poland. The Summer Olympics), our educational output (the kind of people that would actually elect the administration), etc., our best bet was to actively promote these future dictators. They would soon be heading off to very good colleges, every one of them. With their ability to manipulate events in their favor, with their preternatural understanding of human nature, particularly fear and distrust, a proper, indoctrinating education backed by a secret cabal was our only hope. Our last chance to stay in control. I was against the idea in principle, but voted yes because I didn't dare let a nay be put down on the record against those monsters, and because after my divorce to Allison (pants sued off), I wanted to be on the winning side of something.

I would keep coming back to the question that made no sense: why did Lori sleep with me? She was even mostly age appropriate, only three years younger than I was, nothing like my former conquests. The day of our affair, after the decision to straight-up-recruit the Fuhrer Boys, ended with both of us sauced, naked in my office. I decided to keep the streak running, and showed up to work drunk for a week before I was shipped off to rehab, placed on administrative leave, with Lori taking over my position.

*

The rehab facility was nice. Really nice. I was there for a little more than a year. This was Michigan, near Lake Superior, and it had the only pine trees I'd seen in nearly twenty years. I'd forgotten that places like that even existed anymore; how could an area of such beauty be possible when nearly the rest of the world was burning? I didn't interact with people very much, most conversations consisting of the clichés of group therapy, but my life felt suddenly like its own conversation. This is my body, I was saying. If I wanted, I could simply forget everything else. So I did. It was the new American Dream.

I would climb the hill just beyond the tree line behind the facility and stare at the last major body of water in the United States. I would watch the birds escape north into Canada and wonder if they were following migratory patterns or if they had sensed that this was their last chance.

The people below, in the lakeside town, drove their ratty pickups along the winding roads, resembling in their activity a hive of ants. It seemed like they were oblivious to the economic magnifying glass aimed upon their colony. Or maybe I was just looking down on them like a prideful alcoholic on a hill. They would all be driven from their town soon anyways, displaced by the escalating property taxes as the powerful men and women drove out the natives into their trailer parks in western Nebraska.

When I returned from my extended time away, the workplace I had known no longer existed. Lori explained to me as best she could the orders that had come from above, the need to get the Fuhrer Boys into positions of actionable power as soon as possible. I was still focusing on me, on staying sober and I couldn't, or wouldn't understand exactly why the speed was necessary. The world had changed and I was oblivious. I was no longer part of the plan. At least I couldn't make things worse. I was put in a basement and given the task of running chemical analysis on thousands of vials of genetic material.

This lasted four years. I learned to cook a little, I streamed a lot of comedy, I calculated the odds of a nuclear suppression in the event of a popular uprising (seventy eight percent, plus or minus two), marked the areas safest from fallout. I kept myself busy with not drinking.

Then I got a knock on my door from Lori while I was making dinner. She was almost fifty then, but she still looked good. I was fifty two myself and I had no real recollection of getting old. I couldn't even imagine how I looked to her. I'd halfheartedly believed that the rest of the world had grown younger while I continued eternally as myself. It took an old affair to remind me of my mortality. I must have stood at the door for longer than I imagined, because Lori invited herself in.

There was grimness in her eyes, a deadening I understood. "Been watching the news?"

I hadn't, I had dinner to finish. It was nothing special, lamb chops with a pistachio tapenade, something that took a little over fifteen minutes to prepare, but looked like it required real time and skill. I'd only just finished the tapenade, only just heated the skillet, so I added a second chop to the pan for the company.

"It isn't good," Lori said while I worked on the food. "We're falling behind, we're being eaten up."

Instead of responding, I tried to remember what Lori had looked like naked, but my recollection could only come to a hazy approximation. If I could take off her clothes again it would all come back to me, but I would have to make do until then with the curves of her against the strain and the push of fabric, her slightly shoddy powersuit, the way it pressed her into a shape that was both hers and not. Sure, the world as we knew it was ending, but I had been clean for half a decade, I hadn't had sex in a year and I hadn't eaten in eight hours. You have to take things as you take them. Nothing else much amounts to anything.

I pulled the lamb from the oven, served the meat out on two white plates with a helping of coleslaw. I looked at Lori frankly, this time for what and who she actually was, not trying to glimpse her nude form underneath, not trying to make this picture a fantasy of who I wanted her to be. I took her all in, from the strong shoulders and powerful face to the slightly defeated bend in the belly. It was a picture I didn't know the title to. Something I couldn't put my finger on, but knew I needed to take the time to think of something. I pulled out my bottle of emergency scotch and poured her a glass.

"Should you have that in your house?" She said.

"You should always be prepared to make mistakes."

Lori took her glass and smiled. We took our plates to

the dining room. I sipped my little glass of water with an approximation of a smile, even though the Oban seared my nostrils with the urgency of a two o'clock invitation.

She never actually told me what she had really come over to say. Something terrible, no doubt. We just finished our dinner and then she left. She came by the next night, though, and the next, and we talked about things that didn't really matter. It was strange the way she would just stand and watch me while I prepared the food, but it felt good. Why, specifically, her gaze was different than the mandatory cameras all over my house I couldn't exactly say.

Lori moved in right as the Fuhrer Boys came into real power. It turns out the Stalins and Napoleons were relatively benign on their national perches, just having that control was enough for them. Or maybe it's just the lull before apocalypse. It seems inevitable if you ask me. Until then, we let ourselves be watched, we obey the voices from the screen, we heed the prodding shocks on the street, we do the work required to maintain the bureaucracy, but when we are home and we get that feeling, as everyone does, that we are being watched, at least there is a friendly face when we turn around, smiling, helping us to forget the world we created. Maybe it's more than we deserve. But it's what we have.

Body, Etc.

To say that I will never forget is to imply that it could ever be an option. Like all great tragedies, it began so simply. A cold. After an entire month in the confines of other human beings, whether that is the hermetic enclosure of transport, or even just the cold of winter driving everyone together around warmth, one can never really undo the sneezes and touches and breath-on-face of close company. Probably everyone around me got sick that month. The difference was: they got better.

So I get a cold, which I tell Erin isn't a problem, really, and I push on. And somehow that becomes pneumonia, because I won't rest, because I have work to do, and it lingers on the periphery for so long that the disease just outlasts my immune system. The pneumonia becomes septic, which is less fun than it sounds: and that is considering its lingering associations with septic systems, whereby you run a drainage system through your yard so that your shit and piss will fertilize the root system of your grass. And then, when I finally come out of the woods from the pneumonia and the sepsis, comes the C-Dif, which is when your body gives up entirely and the bacterial colony living in your gut throws up its hands and goes on strike, refusing to process what comes through while you contract in spasms of pain, wasting, taking off those inches around the belly you wanted gone, and then the inch you didn't even secretly hope you could be rid of, and then that inch you didn't know was possible to lose and that you want back, truly, because now you're turning into some pale shadow of yourself, and literally melting away because of a 12th century condition.

The good news is that when you go through this kind of suffering and watch your body go from plump to thin to emaciated, you get to try every possible combination of drugs, and regale your friends and family into submission with their names (generic and trade) and doses, and the ways in which they do not help.

And then Erin steps in and berates the doctors for so long that they go back to their MD 101 manuals and set up a fecal transplant. It isn't as gross as it sounds, but does require Erin to shit into a cup and for that to be turned into a small handful of pills which the doctor and nurse, and pharmacist, and gastroenterologists (Attending and Resident and Intern and gaggle of visiting students) assures you, assures you, will taste like nothing, and will not break open until they are safely into your gut. The first series of pills send you into bedpan suffering as the last batch of idle bacteria are tossed on their goddamned heels, and then you get the second batch, where your wife's shit replaces your own.

What does it feel like? Immediately, it feels like nothing. A few days later, it feels like you're finally getting better.

How else does it feel? You are literally colonized. Your shit is no longer your own. Your bacteria are now in sync with the donor, and you thank god it's your wife, because you don't know what it would be like to be transformed from the inside out by some stranger. What if you didn't share political views? Heaven forbid.

I keep saying you. I mean I. It's just—

How does it feel? Well, you get your shit together. And then, three days after the transplant, when you are recovered enough for the immediate stress to dissipate and for your wife to feel comfortable enough to fight with you over this or that rude thing you have said or done over the last two weeks of agony, you can say to her something unfair, and she will say:

Erin

I never said that. I just think that there is a better way to handle the whole fucking affair, is all.

You (me)

You know what the most enlightening part of this whole fecal transplant is? I've have definitive proof that despite your claims to the contrary, your shit really *does* stink Erin. It really does, and maybe you just can't tell for your high goddamned horse.

Erin

Nice.

You (me)

Oh, and you're too good for comebacks too. Wouldn't want to muck about with us peasants in the pettiness of insults.

Erin

That's not. I'm sorry. I'm just trying to talk.

Me (you)

Etc., etc.

Erin

Etc.

You (me)

Etc.

Erin

Etc. (leaves the room)

And then you get checked out of the hospital, and you begin recovering and then you're better and you go about your life, and you find that there is some sort of a wedge between you two that hadn't existed before, even though you are closer than ever, having suffered such a harrowing experience, where you glimpsed down the hallway of the abyss and saw that there was nothing but darkness and she saw her life as your widow unfolding, and so you are squeezing each other harder and harder together, feeling the warmth, the softness and security of your bodies, the ways in which you mould, perfectly or imperfectly depending on mood and the shift of the body, but belonging together. Only now there is that thing there, that pebble, round and hard, like an obsidian chickpea and you don't like that it is there (or maybe you are only just now feeling it after a decade of marriage because you are so much closer now, because of the near-death, etc.), but there is nothing to do but go on.

And you go on. You bicker, you love. Go to work and return to each other. I. Me. I go to work, I get promoted, I take on more responsibility, but make sure not to neglect home. We get on. We have a great life. We decide children aren't for us, but we mentor, we support, we volunteer. There is some greater meaning other than just the pleasures of the body and the mind.

*

And then one goes to the doctor and there is an x-ray, and the doctor says to such a person that there is a dark spot—a blotch—and a person, a normal, average person who has led a relatively successful and happy life, who has had their share of sadness and tragedy, may be staggered by such an ominous sentence because they know through medical television shows what blotches really mean and that it is not something at all related to shady optics and that this kind of uncertainty is certainty itself.

One. I mean you. I mean I. I tell the doctor that this isn't really possible because haven't I already been through enough with the cold that became every other worst possible scenario with the sepsis and the C-Dif and the nearly dying? I mean, you haven't even really put the weight back on, and even then, every pound goes to some sort of bulging, alien sack instead of filling out your body like it used to, like it is supposed to, so that instead of being voluptuous you just have a pot.

The doctor smiles at you and tells you that she just wants to run a check, and then she and the other doctor, the doctor called in for the blotch who you trust as much as the very word blotch, they tell you that they just want a biopsy, and while the other doctor (the blotch doctor, who has a kind of razor smile that tells you that the cutting is her favorite part) is off running results, your own doctor comforts you, with a dead-faced pose of certainty, assuring you that things will not be like the C-Dif, which was unlucky and horrible, but even that went fine, in the end. This will be better, she assures you.

It isn't better though. One finds out that it is a rare form of bone cancer. One learns the name. One learns that it has no actual Latin name or even a nickname because just one thing to call it is enough. One learns how others refer to it. Unlucky is a word. One learns many things.

One goes to appointments and receives jabs and treatments dripped from toxic bags. One makes progress, but at the expense of one's own body. It begins to fall apart. Traitor. One can no longer eat almonds because the salt and the chemical aftertaste of the nut is a reminder of the way in which one can "taste" the saline they prep an IV with. The weight drops again, but this time because of neglect. Because one cannot be bothered. Because if one's body will fail, such that the head goes from luscious to bare, because if one's body creates pain on the inside, because one's body multiplies pain at a rate that must be met with even more pain—well. Well then the body doesn't deserve anything, and one damned well won't force oneself into this something-else of feeding it and caring for it, this traitor.

One's "good" doctor says things are progressing well and the dark spots are receding, and then the good doctor is gone, flying away in total defeat. Then the shark-toothed doctor shoves her vicious leer into one's face and snaps out that speech that was always coming about complications that one had already read about on the wire, as one does, studying the possibilities for the worst to come down to, almost like a wish, with one's kenner and computer, with one's eyeballs practically pulling themselves out of their sockets so that they may meet the light emitted from the little light emitting diodes just a fraction of a second sooner. It is one of those appointments.

Of course, one says to the doctor with the sharp teeth. Of course there is death to meet the cancer. The cancer would not go willingly alone. The shark doctor lays out the schedule and the procedure, and the plan is to finish with the chemo and the radiation and to lay waste to the system entirely, to rid the body once and for all (or for a few years, the sharktor caveat emptors) of that too-prosperous cell block, taking with it the bone sponge it suckled on, and then following that myeloablative shock, the allogeneic donor will give their marrow, for one's own will be bleached dead and dry from the intensity of x- and gamma rays shined into one and the chemical wasteland still ravaging one's cells. Then that donor tissue will be injected (hypoallogeneic?) and one will be all better again.

Shark

Easy as pie

One (you (me (I plus my wife's shit)))
Where the hell do you get *your* pies?

One's wife agrees. She nods sympathetically and holds one's hand. She will cry, later, but right then, and suddenly, Erin decides to act rather chipper about the situation. Of course she is the donor. Of course. One can barely even feel the chickpea at times, but it is always there. Before the operation she jokes about the ridiculous succession of donations in the most good-natured way possible.

Erin
You really can't get enough of me, can you?

You (me(I plus Erin's Shit) (one))
Etc.

*

And the operation goes swimmingly. A body heals. One heals. You heal. I heal. I scream for icecream. A body heals. It takes what it has been given and it goes with it. It bucks and it reacts, but after time, after healing, after drugs and the prayers of an atheist body which believes in wanting to live, it begins its haemopoiesistic process and the body is flooded with another body's blood. A body is even more a chimerical body. A body no longer digests itself, it no longer bleeds itself. It digest and bleeds other. It digests and bleeds Erin. A body is now the old body and Erin. Body + Erin = Berin? Barren? Bare and?

A body
Do you know how much I love you? If you cut me, I bleed Erin. Not even a homicide detective with an entire lab team could tell us apart. That's love.

Erin
Unless they did a cheek swab or took a hair sample or—

A body
I mean, if you enjoy killing jokes, that isn't necessarily *wrong*, per se—

A wife
That is funny because the word killing and the context of a homicide detective.

                              A body
Etc.

                              Erin
Etc.

Tell a body: what do you know of iodinated radiographic contrast media? I knew nothing of the sort, you understood that it helped the technicians find out the fine details of what was happening in the body, one understood that it was painful and a body knows that in sufficient doses it puts an incredible strain upon the kidneys.

                              Erin
Whatever we need to do, we do it.

                              A body
—

                              Erin
It's fine. It's fine. We'll be fine.

                              A body
—

                              Erin
Ericka, listen. Listen. It's not even the worst thing that's happened so far. I mean, hell, those fuckers are basically disposable, right?

A body laughs when dark humor hits home, but doesn't agree with the sentiment. A body knows that it needs kidneys. It needs them like it needs a liver that is wasted in this period of prolonged abstinence. It knows that it needs kidneys more than it does tear ducts, and even those have been malfunctioning, leaving a body's eyes dry when they needed moisture to focus and flooded when they needed the clarity just to—

There is no more Sharktor, she has smiled her last toothy grimace and moved on to extract and to cut on others, to savor the smell of applied nuclear energy on the frail bodies of other bodies. A body has a new doctor, an elderly one, who explains the causes that have already been explained.

Doctor
Unfortunately, any number of things can lead to an acute event. Contrast, in certain doses, diabetes, external crushing trauma—

Erin
So, wait. Should I not have been going straight to kidney punches whenever I got stressed out?

Doctor
(The silence that makes a body wonder what calculations are being made regarding legal liability and obligation and the kinds of slack that should be given to the family of those who have suffered and the responsibilities to the patient and to the referring doctor and to the hospital and—)

Erin
It's. Uh. A joke. It's—funny?

A body
Because the joke is abuse. And the humor lies in the fact that abusers rarely articulate the exact nature of their abuse, especially unbidden in an environment where there are personal and professional obligations for such instances to be reported to the proper authorities.

                        Doctor
(The silence that makes a body wonder if the
doctor is actually an artificial vehicle for an alien
or computer intelligence and dealing here with its
very first instance of humor within the confines of
the white walled hospital).

                        Erin
And what's really funny is that we *fucking know* that
it is you and this *fucking hospital* and the fucking
doctor with the teeth—

                        A body
The sharktor—

                        Erin
And the whole goddamned process of raining
down chemo and radiation like it's a nineteen forties
nuclear runoff water lawn-sprinkler celebration
and we're trying to do our best to deal with the
stress of another goddamned operation with little
to no chance of—

                        Erin
(Malfunctioning tear ducts)

                        Doctor
(Etc.)

                        A body
Etc.
                          *

A body has blood pumped through a machine. A body
goes on lists. A body attends meetings and appointments,
and a body is canceled on and shuffled around and promised
to and. And. And. A body waits outside while Erin fills out
forms. A body feels for the chickpea, the obsidian one. It
pulses. Erin takes care of everything. A body waits and

while it waits it wilts again. A body gets a go ahead. A body receives the notification to count from ten, and sees the doctor looming overhead, waiting for zero. A body is going to make an inappropriate joke to the doctor about a flight of stairs, but the countdown is already taking the first step, to nine, and the body is unconscious.

*

Time jumps. The container is a year older. Healthy. Everything functions as it should, allowing for the fact that everything does so in a physical location it shouldn't function in.

Erin

You are not "a container."

A container

Easy for you to say. You're not the walking storage shed. Neighbor, can I borrow a lung next time, perhaps?

Erin

You're not a container. Be a little more fair to yourself. You're *at least* a climate controlled storage unit.

A climate controlled storage unit

I stand corrected.

*

Time jumps. A container is sick of being cared for. It no longer needs such concerns. When the container holds Erin, it can barely contain the obsidian, a grapefruit. Erin's favorite snack is almonds. She would give them up if a container asks. A container holds, and is responsible for holding. As long as the container exists, it succeeds.

Erin

Bullshit. And you're not even maintaining all that
well. I still have to remind you to take your meds.

A container

Ten minutes late isn't late.

Erin

Tell that to your boss.

A container

That's the point. This is the kind of argument you
have with your boss, not your wife.

Erin

Not again.

A container

Etc.

Erin

Etc.

*

Time jumps. Obsidian. When is gratitude resentment?

A container

Etc.

Erin

Etc.

A container

Etc.

Erin

I still love you. I haven't stopped.

A container

Do you? It feels more like you've just invested too

much to stop—

> Erin

I *have* invested a lot, but that's not—

> A container

Etc.

> Erin

Etc.

> A container

That's not fair.

> Erin

None of this is fair.

> Erin

—Etc. —

> A container

—Etc. —

> Erin

Fine. Fine. Here you go. You have it. Call off the hounds.

> A container

I'm sorry.

> Erin

(Faulty Tear ducts)

> A container

(Faulty Tear ducts)

> Etc. Etc.

*

A day passes. A container is in an accident. A nurse at the emergency room makes a kind and a sardonic gesture:

Nurse
I thought we told you that you weren't welcome here anymore.

Etc. Laughing. Tear ducts. The works. The hand has to be amputated. Etc. A five star safety rating only means: on average. A container knows how a container can fail. The car did what it could. A container did what it could. Good is not always good enough. So it goes. The hand. Etc.

Erin happens to be in the field. Erin happens to have been in the field the entire time, but it was never relevant. A story holds even the stories it didn't tell. A biomechanical engineer. A worker of hands. She works tirelessly. Even though the divorce is final. She puts herself in charge of the project. She lends a hand to a Container. A body. Etc. She is in charge of the mechanical systems, the servos and carbon fiber ligaments. She does not write the software. She does not sculpt the design. She only lends a hand. Still she is in charge. The hand does not look like a hand, it looks like something more severe. Hand crafted, though. Severe is good.

The hand is good. It is not *as* good. It hurts. But it is good. It is a replacement, and replacements are not of the body. The body is no longer the container. The body is no longer a body, a cyborg; it is stitched together flesh, a Frankenstein; it is something else. It is become.

I thank Erin personally for all of her work. (Faulty tear ducts). She invites me for a drink. She proposes calibration exercises involving glassware and then more tender vessels.

(Faulty tear ducts). Etc. We talk. Etc. She says maybe we're too alike. But it isn't that, is it? The obsidian is gone, but in its place, the body, my body—the I—is something different.

Erin

—Etc.—you still have my heart.

Me

(Faulty tear ducts). Can we not make any more organ jokes, please?

When she asks why (the big one, the real one), I don't have a reason. I have so many of them. But none of them are because of the body, my body, her body. They are more mundane. There is something else. There is the obsidian and there is its lack. She knows it too. Maybe she likes that. To fill the lack. Maybe I am broken. I owe her my body. She tells me not to forget her. (Faulty tear ducts). I nod and walk away. To imply that I even could is—Etc.

I go home and grab a whiskey glass. I grip it in my new hand, but the calibration isn't quite right and it shatters before I can get it to my face.

Etc.

Clearing

October 8th, 2005

Staring into the stars, John wonders if he would have sex with an alien. Would they even look like us, or would they have beaks and tentacles, grasping phalanges in areas they ought not to? Would aliens find some pathetic Earthling attractive? Would everything fit? How strange to get to the moment of truth and—what would he say in that situation? Would "I'm sorry" cover it? "I swear I've never had incompatible organs before." Perhaps there were intergalactic laws against behavior of that sort. Penal Code 4372197.013, Section B: No Screwing the Earthlings.

Penal code.

Eddie said he'd meet at ten, but it's nearly ten fifteen. John lounges on the soft grass, takes in the smell of the green. The clearing is hidden behind trees, blocking the suburban light; better to see the stars, better to talk, better to hitch a ride off the planet should the opportunity arrive. Eddie's parents seemed to have no problems with him staying out late at night. Probably trying to avoid making the same mistakes they'd made with their older son, the rules and strictness that had blazed a path straight to the Marines.

John's mother would kill him if she caught him out so late; she would spank him and ground him for a week; she would remove his favorite books from his room so the punishment really sank in. She would lecture him about how she worries, that she needs to know where he is. She would make a face like it pained her more than him. John scans the horizon, the dark silhouettes of pine trees, an anomaly in central Ohio, their needles hanging like a hundred-thousand-trillion teeth. The ominous sight betrayed by the sweet tang in the air of sap oozing from the bark. As if, he thinks, his over-protective mom is a kind of maternal mother-ship with a shield of protection that can only be activated when she knows where he is. A mother mother-ship.

He looks at the stars and admires the milky clouds that are millions and billions of stars the same number of light years away. He hopes that there is something out there. Maybe even something that would sleep with him.

At ten thirty Eddie finally shows up, running through the woods, his shadow flickering like a dark strobe against the trees, jumping up their trunks, back down onto the dark grass then back up again

"Man," John says, "where've you been? What if mom checks in on me? If I'm not there—you don't even understand." John winces at the whiny tone of his own small voice.

"Sorry. Dad drove me out to Port Columbus," Eddie says, "Said I should be there."

John can't help but think that he's always the last to know about everything. "What for?"

"Justin's unit came home," Eddie acts nonchalant in a way still impressive and unique to John. "Dad says it's only right for us to welcome them back."

"Oh," is all John can say. He doesn't have the words. Eddie's brother was killed when his Humvee hit a mine in Afghanistan, a country John couldn't locate on a map before the accident. He is still embarrassed by his ignorance. "Um," he says, "did anyone know you were" —he searches to fill the void because—"his family?"

Eddie shakes his head. "Not really. We mostly just shook hands with guys as they got off the plane. A few recognized me from pictures Justin had shown 'em, said hi. They were nice, talked about how great Justin was. I don't know, it was lame, man."

"Um," John says again.

"Yeah."

Eddie's words hang in the clearing like a balloon low on helium. John fidgets, sticks his hands in his pockets. He grabs a quarter from the lint and twirls it around his fingers. Around and around—what the hell is he supposed to say?

October 20th, 2015

"I'm sorry about what happened to your brother," he says to Eddie, a decade late.

"What?" Eddie says. It's the wrong time for John to say this to him: two days before Eddie gets married. They're at the bachelor party. John has pulled Eddie outside to tell him this.

"I never said that to you. Before. I wanted to say the right thing, but I couldn't. I felt like I failed you. It has haunted me."

"You were there," Eddie says, "does anything else matter?" They hug each other until it grows awkward. They've been drinking too much. They let go and stare across the night, craning their necks to the sky.

"The stars are bright, huh?" Eddie says.

"They are." John still hopes, like he did as a kid, that he will see a bright streak across the sky signaling something more than a meteor.

"It brings you back, doesn't it?" Eddie reaches into the air like he could pluck a star from the night and put it in his pocket, just like that. Then he turns and walks back into the bar.

John watches him go, then turns back into the night.

October 8th, 2005

They lie on the grass, watching the stars like they always have, like they know they always will. The black is so deep that John cannot help imagining it is bound tight with dark matter, dense and mysterious, and he becomes afraid that maybe his eyes will be pulled into it like into a black hole, sucked clean from his skull. He knows he's being silly but he can't help closing his eyes. For a full minute. He silently counts one-onethousand, two-onethousand. Eddie points out a shooting star and for a stupid, gullible second, John's prayers have been answered and he is free of his life. "It's beautiful," Eddie says and John is still lying on his back on top of the hill and the light is just a shooting star and John is just a kid with wild fantasies.

"Do you think that God is four dimensional?" John says to Eddie, who doesn't respond. "Do you think he gets to exist outside of time so that he can see all times simultaneously?" Eddie still says nothing. "Sometimes I think that when we die, maybe we'll get to be like that too. Maybe if you can rearrange time, things would make sense."

"That's idiotic," Eddie says. "If you existed at all times simultaneously you wouldn't need to rearrange time, it would all just, you know, be. You could just experience your entire life instead of trying to arrange it as if causality even mattered. The fourth dimension isn't some metaphoric key."

"Shut up," John says.

March 11th, 2024

John gets up early and buys a diamond ring for his girlfriend, Julia. He takes it home and opens the box. The diamond is big; he hopes it will be enough. Julia is beautiful in the way that magazines say women are beautiful and John knows, as surely as he has known anything about women, that his minor financial success is mostly to account for her attraction to him.

He kneels in front of the door when he hears her car pull into the driveway. She takes her time; he hears her opening and closing the car doors, again and again. She's always forgetting things. His knee starts to hurt, the pain beginning to taste like the hardwood beneath him. It takes almost five minutes before she scratches around the lock with her key, finally letting herself in.

Julia is carrying an entire load of groceries; her arms shoved through the canvas bag handles all the way up to her elbows. "Oh my God, John," she says. She lowers herself to the ground with a series of dull thunks as the grocery bags slide off of her arms.

"Will you marry me?" No preamble, no speech, just the words.

"I thought you were never going to ask," Julia says. Her eyes twinkle in the light. "I thought I was going to have to be thankful for a key." She leans forward into John and he moves to put his arms around her, snagging himself on the grocery bags so that they are clumped on the floor together: man, woman, kale. She is weeping, not crying. He feels immediately trapped by his future. "Yes, I'll share my life with you," she says. "How long have you been planning this?"

"I couldn't wait."

"I'm glad you didn't."

March 10th, 2024

John finishes reading Eddie's first book. It is a science fiction explosion of memoir and space opera, and it opens him as cleanly as an obsidian blade. In it, Eddie travels back in time to talk to Justin, his dead brother. He fights in the war alongside his brother, soon to perish, they save a great man and unearth a government conspiracy, but really it's about the connection that was severed between them, when Eddie was only a kid, which he has somehow regained in this journey. It is lie after lie stacked into a tower that can only be called the truth. John is overwhelmed by the kind life he hasn't been able to live. Overwhelmed by the idea that there is something he is missing.

October 8th, 2005

"Maybe," John says, "maybe if we didn't have to worry about what comes next we could actually understand what was meant to be."

"Shut up, John," Eddie says. "Please."

John pushes himself onto his elbows, looks at his friend. They are still for a long time.

"I never cried when Justin died," Eddie says and John feels like every possible probability in their friendship stretches out before them at that exact moment. "When Mom told me, it seemed—it's not possible for someone to just *say* something like that and for it to be true."

John nods. "I know," he says, and he means that when his parents told him they were separating, it felt the same way. He hasn't told Eddie about that yet, even if he sometimes means to. But when you're hurting, how do you reach out to other people? How do you let them know that you are vulnerable, and that now would be a good time to strike? Besides, there is still a chance that the divorce will blow over like so many of their fights.

"Then there was the funeral, and Justin was there. Right in front of me. Just—lying. I squeezed my eyes together and I told myself that I had to cry, because if I didn't, everyone would know I was a terrible brother." Eddie looks at John, away from the stars. "I couldn't. Does that make me a terrible person?"

"I didn't cry for almost a month when nana died," John says, looking at the grass. "Then one day I was reading *A Wrinkle in Time* and I just started bawling, even though the book was completely lame." It is a lie. John cried as soon as he heard the news. He was only six and he loved his nana. He thinks the lie sounds right, though—manly and reassuring.

"He was my brother," Eddie says. "He was my brother. Every day I wished he was home. And when I got my wish it was because he's dead."

John feels a perverse envy for Eddie's brother.

"Sometimes," Eddie says, "my mom looks at me and I can tell that she knows something's wrong with me. Like maybe I don't have a soul."

John laughs, the sound coming from nowhere. "Of course you have a soul." He feels wrong for laughing, but he can't help it. He laughs harder.

"Stop laughing, fucker," Eddie says and begins to giggle himself. "What's so damned funny? It isn't funny. You're making me laugh, too. It's sick. You're sick, man."

"I can't help it," John says, trying to stop, which succeeds for a moment before the inappropriate laughter bubbles up again. They take turns calming down and cracking up, they yell at each other, and from a distance they are just thirteen-year-olds, not so serious they can't laugh over tragedy. When they have exhausted themselves, John says, "You're a good brother," and he feels lame for saying it.

"I guess, Jingleheimer," Eddie says.

April 27th, 2002

John and Eddie are in the basement playing Xbox, like practically always. Eddie spends most of his free time hanging out with John since his older brother joined the Marines the month before. Before that, they'd been neighbors, not yet friends. Eddie is winning, like practically always; he shoots John's avatar in the head with a sniper rifle.

Upstairs, John's mother calls for him.

John is too focused to hear. The words wash through him and are forgotten. If he can get to the rocket launcher, he can take out Eddie, the smug jerk. And his little sniper rifle too. His mother calls a second time, which he hears, but he's almost got the shot.

"John Jacob Jingleheimer Schmitt," his mother sing-songs from the top of the stairs. When John was four, it was his favorite nickname. Now it is infuriating, especially with company.

"Don't call me that," John says.

"His name is my name too." Eddie joins in. They are matching sopranos. "Whenever I go out, the people always shout."

"Shut up," John shouts and looks at Eddie with the wounded look he still hasn't learned only encourages bullies and the cruelty of friends. Eddie shakes his head and smiles hard.

"There goes John Jacob Jingleheimer Schmitt."

"Stop it!" John shouts above their voices.

"Lala, lalalalala."

May 2nd, 2005

John is reading his anthology of the year's best science fiction stories when his mom knocks on the door. "Honey," she says, coming in without waiting for an answer. "Eddie is going to come over for a little while."

"Okay," John says. Eddie comes in and John can hear his mother talking to Eddie's parents at the door, voices low in tragedy. "Hey," John says to Eddie.

"Hey," Eddie says.

"What's up?"

"My brother died," Eddie says and John almost says something stupid, like, "I'm sorry."

"Want to play Xbox?"

"Yeah," Eddie says.

October 8th, 2005

To break the silence, John says, "Would you have sex with an alien?"

"What is with your jacked-up brain?

"Well, see," John says, "suppose you get picked up by some aliens and they want to study you or something and you get horny, and, like, they're willing. Maybe that's one of their experiments or something."

"You're disgusting," Eddie says. "Besides, you never know what they're working with. What if there's, like, acid up in there? Shit, I don't think it's worth the risk." Eddie laughs with an adult timbre that John is jealous of. He's been recording himself in an effort to sound cooler, more like Eddie, but his laugh is high and hyena in comparison.

John blushes, embarrassed but undeterred. "Suppose no risk."

"If it's all good to go," Eddie says, "sure, why not? It would make a story."

John says, "Yeah, me too."

"Wait a second, numbnuts, what makes you think *any* species would fuck you?"

"You're a jerk," John says. He wishes he could call Eddie an asshole, but he's no good at swearing like Eddie is, and the attempts always come off like a three-year-old cursing, but not cute.

March 9th, 2024

Eddie is in town with his wife Sarah for the weekend, so John and his girlfriend Julia take them out to dinner. The conversation strays often into the topic of politics, but they are all in agreement, more or less. The girls, new friends over dinner, head to the ladies room before the foursome disbands.

"She's beautiful," Eddie says.

John beams. It's true and he has to bite his tongue to keep from lording it over Eddie. He likes Sarah, and had even harbored a crush some years ago, but he feels special with a girl like Julia. "She is," he says. John feels generous, so he admits more than he usually would. "She's a little vain sometimes, but no one's perfect, right?"

"I can see that," Eddie says, the look on his face trying to signal reluctance to say anything.

John is taken completely off guard. He had expected polite denials, not agreement. Sure, it sometimes annoys him when she needs another five minutes for her hair, as if she isn't so much better than him already. And sometimes he feels like she doesn't get him, underneath everything, but who gets anybody? Fuck Eddie. "Well," he says, hedging.

Eddie's expression is a retracted move in a friendly chess game. For the sake of peace, both players try to pretend it didn't happen. "You're a lucky man. How are your classes? Any promising students?"

Julia and Sarah return to the table before the conversation can right itself, and the effect of having to balance their loved ones is dizzying. "Now's as good a time as ever," Eddie says and his wife puts a book in his hands. John is struck by the magic of the book suddenly existing from nowhere, pulled from her handbag like a well-rehearsed magic trick. "Fresh off the presses, final art and everything. I wanted you to have the first copy. I signed it so it's worth something at least. I'd buy it for a dollar." He grins.

February 17th, 2028

John is miserable at the party for Eddie's second book. His first sold almost a million copies despite nonexistent advertising and the publisher is making up for their lack of faith with an extravagant launch for the follow-up. There is a small circle of people around Eddie, listening to him summarizing their friendship and the story of how he started writing.

"I went off." Eddie tells the crowd and they wait through the pause like a television audience, "I said, 'John, no one cares about science fiction: it's ridiculous and you better give it up if you ever want a girlfriend.' He didn't though, talking about science class and how it was like such and such book, or some story he'd read. When John became a real scientist, it made me remember all of those old stories he would tell me about, and the *real* science behind them. Something clicked. So he went off to make a better world, and I started to write about a fake one. My career is really all John, he did the work." Eddie raises his champagne flute. "I'm just glad copyright law doesn't work that way." Everyone laughs.

Eddie continues talking, but John wanders away from the group. It is a beautiful party: there are white linens over tables with shrimp Alexander, crab cakes, plates of brie shaped like oozing monsters, prosciutto and stacks of crackers, chocolate fountains and elaborate ice sculptures carved into spaceships. There are wireless decorative electric lights attached to dishes and walls, and great strings of soft white bulbs, like pearls, drooping from the ceiling. The whole room glows ivory and yellow and everything metal gleams like the moon on water.

"There you are," Julia says, though he doubts she was really looking for him. She is the kind of woman who moves though a party like a leaf in a stream, briefly staying in a swirling eddy before making her way past and down to the next brief interlude. Sometimes it cannot help but feel that her ability is his inability.

"Here I am," John says.

"Moping again? Wishing you had been the successful writer?"

"Doesn't everyone?"

"Mmm," Julia says. "You're probably right. But so few are. Besides, I've read your stories, love. I've reread them; Eddie is the writer."

John pouts and pulls away. "You wouldn't understand."

"I wouldn't understand what?"

"Nothing." Petulant.

Julia touches his arm. "You can sulk in your study at home and complain that I don't understand you, if you want. Maybe I don't, maybe no one can ever understand another person, but I love you: for who you are, and not for who you wished you might have been in some other life. Hold it against me if you have to, but Christ, John, make an effort to look happy for your friend."

As she walks away, John wishes that instead of astrophysics he had pursued astronomy. Perhaps it isn't too late. If he were an astronomer, he could spend months in the most remote regions of the Earth, not being so confounded, peering into the night sky, searching for supernovas and proof of alien intelligence.

October 8th, 2005

Eddie looks surprised at the revelation. "No homework at all?" he says.

"Not for social studies."

"Just because you're in therapy?"

"Since two weeks ago," John says.

"Such bullshit," Eddie says. "So your dad threw a vase. Hell, my dad throws shit all the time. I can't believe your mom makes you go to that garbage."

John nods and tries not to look guilty. He knows that Eddie will figure it out soon enough that his dad has moved out, they're neighbors after all, but he doesn't want to admit it, not even to Eddie. Acknowledging the possibility is capitulation.

"The first session took longer than I thought it would and I didn't finish my homework. I told Miss Anderson and asked for another day and she just said not to worry about it. She said as long as I didn't tell anyone, I could just have therapy days free."

"Just like that?" Eddie says.

"I think she used to go to therapy when she was a kid or something," John says. "She sometimes looks like she is still very sad."

"God-damn," Eddie says and switches into a falsetto: "'Miss Anderson, I didn't do my homework because my dad threw a vase and it scared me. Boo, hoo, hoo.' I didn't know you were so fucking sly."

"Yeah," John smiles because he's proud of his slyness. He's so *fucking* sly. "I guess I am. Whadayaknow?"

September 23rd, 2005

John can hear his parents shouting up the stairs from his basement room. It is 2:35 in the morning. Through the ceiling they sound muffled, like a *Peanuts* cartoon: "Whaa whaaa, whaawhaaawhaawhaaa." Only in the cartoon, parents never sounded angry. They've been fighting for almost an hour and John needs to pee. He weighs his odds of walking into the argument; he's been there before and won't repeat it.

How long can he hold it before his will gives and he pisses the bed like he's two? Could he just fall asleep in it? Disgusting. He thinks instead how long animals can hold it, or if they even do, unless one believes that birds maliciously wait for Corvettes, as his dad insinuates. How long can aliens go without pissing? Would they even have to? With their superior technology they could probably eliminate the need completely. The idea appeals.

When the pressure of need on his bladder outweighs his qualms, John makes his way, slowly, up the stairs, careful not to step on a creaky board. Don't let them hear. As he nears the door, his parents become less muffled, and almost coherent. Don't let them hear. John just wants to get to the bathroom and back to bed. He stops at the top of the stairs and sticks his tongue out in a false gag at the smell of beets that still lingers from dinner. He listens for location: if he can tell where they are, then he can choose the opportune time to make a run for the bathroom.

"You fucking liar," his mother screams, suddenly next to the door, smelling of liquor and perfume. "Why don't you just tell me the truth about where you were? Asshole." She's far enough gone that her S's sound like slippery T's.

John knows this argument, he's heard it before. It entails a secretary and the "one time." It involves a back and forth of sobbing, screams and invectives.

The sounds of footsteps move to the kitchen. John opens the door to make his run for it.

"Fuck you," his mom says. John can't help looking and then he's trapped. She's sobbing, her mascara reduced to thick smudges, her face red and bloated. She's standing in her bra and underwear. John can't look away from her flesh, sagging slightly, her skin blotchy and pinked. She doesn't even look like his mother anymore. She picks up a handful of mail as she yells, throws it at John's father, though it falls short. "Fuck you," she grabs an apple and lets it fly, hitting him in the chest. "Fuck you," she picks up a can opener.

"You better put that down," John's dad says. He lifts his large hand slowly and points it at her. He is still in his suit, minus jacket, his tie halfway unknotted. His eyes are fierce and tired.

"You don't get to say anything about what I 'better' do. You've lost that right." Her voice has lost the edge of anger; she's calming down.

She throws the can opener.

It hits his father's face below the eye, cutting a red crescent. He doesn't move. The echo of metal on hardwood. Tears run down her face, blood down his.

John's father picks up a vase of flowers and throws it, above her shoulder. It shatters. The impact sounds like a diver touching the water, following through—clear past the surface and into the blue—all that's left is the splash. The shattered vase bursts away from the cabinet, a sphere of water and glass, reflecting a rainbow, raining down drops and shards on John's mother, on his father, on the counter, on the floor. It sounds like a waterfall, like music, like someone should be recording it right now. The flowers get stuck on the cabinet handle and stay upright, suspended, refusing to come down.

John's mother is screaming but he can't hear it, he can only see her mouth hanging, her arms and shoulders ribbon-red, the grotesque bulge of his father's eyes, the monstrosity of his figure. John makes his run for the bathroom before his bladder explodes. He doesn't flush, doesn't wash his hands, just rushes down the stairs and into bed.

March 9th, 2028

Julia talks and John can hear. She asks and he responds. He questions and she answers. They make notes on a piece of paper. Promises. They cross out and add. They sign it together.

Julia puts the paper on the fridge and John smiles at her like he thinks he should and he doesn't know, he really doesn't know how this kind of a thing is supposed to work. He has no model.

"You don't have to understand," Julia says. "You only have to try."

October 8th, 2005

Eddie stands up to go home. He says, "What do you really think happens when we die?"

"I don't know," John says. "Go to heaven and play the harp. I don't know."

"A harp?" Eddie says. "I'll be fucking Megan Bishop from fourth period. That's what I'll be doing."

"I don't know," John says, "that's just what they say. I'd rather do Megan Bishop, though."

"I'll let you have Tabitha," says Eddie. "How about that."

John fake smiles a big, ugly smile. "You're a pal."

"I gotta get home," Eddie says.

John says, "Yeah, me too. I'll see you at school."

"Everything is cool? You know, with your folks and all? I know they, you know."

"Yeah," John is a terrible liar. "Just a bunch of crap."

"Right? I'll see you tomorrow."

John walks home thinking about black holes and singularities. He would like to go through a black hole to see what's on the other side.

At home, his dad's Corvette still isn't in the driveway. He sneaks back into his room, and climbs into his bed. He thinks of a good idea for a story: An intrepid space explorer boldly bravely goes through a black hole and comes out through a singularity. It was actually a wormhole! On the other side, girls grow like apricots and are perfect and willing. He takes one of the girls back through the wormhole/singularity/black hole using apricot-people technology to escape the event horizon of the black hole and is a hero on the other side. Unfortunately, the apricot girl gets moldy and the wormhole closes up so he can't go and pick another one. He's still a hero though, and that's what really matters. He tells himself to try and remember to write the idea down in the morning. He forgets that it is an idea he has stolen.

John misses the sound of his dad in the house, but he can't remember what that is exactly. He thinks about how sound doesn't function in a vacuum and that's why derivative horror movies always try and steal that line about how in space no one can hear you scream.

Re Member

Unstuck from time like Billy Pilgrim I simultaneously witness all pasts and all presents and all futures. I am being beaten up for my strangeness, my inability to communicate properly. There are four of them and they push me around a circle like a bad adaptation of West Side Story; they grow meaner and angrier for reasons I never understand. Eric Willcott throws the first punch and they go wild.

I am being diagnosed by Frankie Munic's father. Eidetic. It is a few years before Frankie will participate in my beating. I understand the diagnosis, but not the facial expression on Mr. Munic's face. Frankie will be the one to out me, so to speak, suffering from a disability is a crime when you are fifteen and strange.

I am At Will Bennet's funeral. His wife refuses to talk to anyone and sits in the corner of the house, weeping. Will was hit by a car and I weep for him. I am accepting Will's apology for the attack a week ago. I am attending Will's wedding. I am accepted into his small circle of friends. I am looking up Will's name when I hear that he is going to the same college as me and I am calling him and he is telling me we should get together for drinks.

I am striking out with Marcus' sister, Mary, and she is laughing at me. "Hey Marcus," she's saying. "Queery McGee just asked me out." I am trying to walk away as Marcus is laughing and telling her she just broke my heart. I am being kicked by Marcus and he is telling me to stay the fuck away from his sister. I am hearing that Marcus manages Vince's, an Italian restaurant outside of Seattle with chocolate cheesecake I think divine. I am running into Mary and she is saying how good it is to see me.

I am taking my car in for body work, the old man greeting me is Thomas Abbott. I am an old man too and it has been more than forty years since he saw me last. He isn't saying anything about that afternoon and neither am I.

I am hearing that Eric joined the Marines and is something of a hero.

I am watching them look at me with eyes of adolescent rage and I am watching them look at me with eyes of regret or anger—how could I have triggered that thing inside of them? I am watching them piece together the past. I am living the past. I am accepting their apologies as they are punching me in the stomach, I am paying them for their services as they are kicking me in the back. They are remembering and I am experiencing. Is this fair? They are asking me if I ever think about that day; I am saying no. I am not telling them that I'm living it right then. This is not fair for anyone.

Memory is an Elephant

Ada heard his voice in the crowd at the open-air market that Saturday afternoon. It was the same crowd she saw everywhere. She hurried through, touching people on the shoulder politely to let them know she was shoving them out of her way and would they kindly comply. Past the fishmongers she walked, past the booths selling baubles for children, past the smell of fresh bread. "Charlie?" said Ada into the crowd, as if the people were trees and the crowd was a forest, as if Charlie lost to the darkness and she the rescue party. "Charlie?"

"Ada?" said the voice, he still unseen. "Can it really be you?"

She parted the crowds with her hands, slipping through with the ease of a young child lost to worried parents. She came across an old man wearing curiously dark spectacles. They were opaque like welding goggles and wrapped around even the sides of his head. His eyebrows raised above the rims in an expression of surprise. "You had better be blind," said Ada. If it was Charlie, he had gotten old and fat. "I don't think I can excuse your taste in eyewear otherwise."

The blind man smiled and it was like the harsh stick of time, beating out the youth of him, had chanced to strike his eyes; it seemed too much, too unfair. She could think of him only as the blind man. "I didn't have you, dear," said he, "to help choose a more attractive blindfold."

"A blindfold is already a better idea," said Ada, snatching at his glasses. His eyes moved like a typewriter, from left to right, punctuated with miniscule pauses, as if considering between keystrokes, before the next letter could hammer down. The eyes moved completely right, stopped for a full second, returned to the left, began their journey again. "You are a writer," said she of his nystagmus. "You must be. It would be brilliant."

"I'm afraid not," said he, taking the glasses back, replacing them on his head. "My eye stutter is a metaphor with no corollary. It merely exhausts my face."

"Too bad."

"I seem to remember," said the blind man.

"I find that hard to believe," said she.

"Of course you're right."

Ada took hold of his left arm. In his right hand was a cane that was not white and did not have a red tip. "Let's get out of this crowd," said she, feeling like a jellyfish among the waves, about to be beached. "I need to get off of my feet."

With the blind man at her side, Ada did not need to touch and weave and push through the crowd—they spread for Charlie automatically, even though the sole hint to his condition was the eyewear he wore, they seemed to know. It parted for he and she, like he was Moses and they a sea, the hand of God reaching down, like cataracts were a disease they were afraid of catching. Who knew? Ada did not believe in God or Moses or phobias.

Ada never talked while walking; she preferred to concentrate on her footsteps, each one bringing her closer to the end of her life, each clipclipclip to be cherished if only because it was the last in a way. And so they passed on through the crowd in silence. A group of children, at least a few dozen of them, though who could tell exactly, were holding wooden toy propellers in their hands attached to a single shaft of wood in the middle that they clasped between their palms. The children counted to three then rubbed their hands together like dismissing a prayer, giving spin to the shaft, giving spin to the propeller, giving energy to the mass that became acceleration that Ada watched lifting out of their hands and into the cloudy, godless sky. Ada pointed at the perpendicular propellers against the grey backdrop of afternoon moisture and the blind man tilted his head, knowing where she pointed even though she walked silently by his side, knowing that the young would replace them even though they didn't need replacement. They were not done yet.

The duo found an empty table at a quiet café, but got nothing to drink. A familiar action, easy to fall into, like the remembrance of youths past. The proprietor brought coffee anyways. They paid and drank to the impotence of not ordering and the ceaselessness of the future: how it heeded them no mind.

"You can't be Charlie," said Ada. "Charlie was young and thin. Charlie could see."

"You can't be Ada," said the blind man. "Ada was young and beautiful. She didn't dawdle on the obvious."

"How would you know if I were young or beautiful, or not?" said Ada.

"Your voice," said the blind man. "You have the voice of an old woman, either made of all fat and sag and full of unwelcome *bons mots*; or too thin, all tendons and fingernails and critical remarks."

Said Ada with a huff, tapping on the metal table, "What ever happened to our dreams of immortality?"

"Dead and buried, so don't muck about the grave," said the blind man. He stood up, bumping the table with his gut, throwing his cane to the ground. It clattered on the concrete, jammed itself between the legs of the far chair. He got onto his knees and clambered after it.

"You seem older and fatter and blinder than ever," said Ada.

"You," said the blind man as he grunted, reaching under the table for his cane, "seem shriller."

Ada trilled like a starling as the blind man grabbed her ankle. This is to say she let out an abrupt cry of startling sharpness. The blank faces of the crowd turned toward her. Of course, all were different, all with noses and eyes and eye teeth of shapes and sizes unique, but one knows that doesn't matter. Just a crowd, they couldn't help but be the same, like rhododendrons in a field of rhododendrons.

"I thought," said the blind man to the crowd from his cave underneath the table, "that her leg was my cane."

Ada gave a thin, colporteur smile. The crowd turned their faceless faces back into each other's backs, back to seeking out baubles for the children and the fanciful displays of acrobatics from the fishmongers. The blind man found his cane and got onto his feet again.

"Come," said the blind man, gathering himself and striding away. "We had better be moving."

"Aren't we always," said Ada. "Where shall we go?"

"Forward," said he. "Come."

"HA," said Ada, her laugh, a single breath exhaled and halted. "The blind leading the—" She faltered. "I'm sure there is an appropriate colloquialism."

They walked towards downtown, working through the throngs, but the crowds only worsened as they neared the heart of the concrete city. Skyscrapers above them proved up to the task of their name and Ada imagined that there were hordes of the crowd looking down from their wall-sized windows down at her, their hands on the glass and their noses smooshed into the panes, their gazes on the top of her head like rays of sun, burning and bearing. Ada flustered at the thought, lost track of her footsteps, came to a stop and tried to calculate where she had been, what she had left. "I wish I had a hat," said Ada when she could take no more.

"I recall," said the blind man.

"You do no such thing," said Ada.

They walked on in silence until they reached the center of the city, where stood a fountain in a square. Concrete nymphs sprung from the concrete street and bent themselves over the water piped in from the sewage plant not more than a mile away. The water spilled from the top of stacked concrete steps, from a hole in the top, and flowed down like the passage of time, uneven and turbulent, pooling at the bottom, draining into pipes and flowing all the way to the processing plant to be mixed with and then separated from shit and piss and paint thinner and battery acid and vomit and stale beer poured straight from aluminum cans, and so on, a myriad myriads of waste until it flowed again into the concrete city, cold and crystalline.

"How long has it been," said the blind man, taking a seat on the edge of the fountain, "since I last saw you?"

Ada also took a seat. "How long has it been since you last saw?" said she, tapping on his glasses.

"When my grandfather died," said the blind man. "He told me, just before, he told me that every sweet thing he had known was dead, had grown old, had become something else entirely—every memory a reminder of endings, an ending of itself."

"Your grandfather couldn't even remember his name," said Ada. "Couldn't find his keys, his spectacles, his slippers, his watch, his wife, his wallet, his testicles, his way around the house; not without a reminder."

"That," said the blind man, "was his genius. He said in such a way he would live forever."

"A fitting philosophy for a dead man," said Ada.

"It must have been years since I last saw you, decades at least. Maybe days, perhaps centuries, or eons."

"It would not," said Ada, "be too hard to imagine leaps as that. I am not the keeper of such things you know. It jumps, erratic and schizophrenic. It gets up and it takes your little neck." She paused, looked at the blind man. "Charlie had a beautiful neck, so lithe and slender," said she.

"Ada had a beautiful voice," said the blind man, "so tender and to the point."

"It takes you by your neck, anyways; maybe a slender neck or that of an obese turkey. It takes your neck and it throttles you and when you come around, you're in disarray and you can't help but feel you've been taken advantage of."

"One could argue," said the blind man, "that you are complicit in the affair."

"That is blaming pregnancy on the growth," said Ada. "Of course it's complicit, the only alternative is—"

The blind man attempted to walk away while she spoke, but he slipped on a wet patch. His cane flew from his hand, his feet from his center of gravity. "Whoops," said the blind man in the air. "Oof," said he from the ground. The crowds made way, a berth with room to spare, in case he should try to stand and accidentally stumble their way.

"Your grasp on that cane," said Ada. "Your grip on that stick of yours is as sure as your perception of light."

The blind man brought his finger to his lips. "Shush," said he.

"You look like a child naming shapes of the clouds."

"I'm watching the space where god used to be."

"In the sky, or in your eyes?"

The blind man continued to lie on his back for quite some time, Ada standing over him, the crowd still bending around them.

"Aren't you tired?" said Ada, "Doesn't it nag at you?"

"Nag?" said the blind man, "only you."

Ada laughed, "HA," and reached down her hand to pick up the blind man. They shuffled like children dancing for the first time until he was on his feet and in possession of his cane once more. They continued their walk through the city. The skyscrapers continued to fulfill their duty; the crowd continued to throng.

"In which direction did we begin?" The question from the blind man.

"Forward," said Ada.

"It sounds like we have returned," said the blind man, "which precludes a straight path."

"All roads bend," said Ada, "of course you know that."

"It seems all circles," said the blind man.

"Isn't it?"

They walked through the stalls, into the smells and the sounds of the day. "What time is it?"

"Later," said Ada. "It is the future."

"Only the present exists," said the blind man. "The future is a wish that will go astray; the past is reconstruction bound by agreed upon points and therefore patently false."

"I am the one who told you that," said she.

"You did say foolish things," said he.

Ada looked through the crowd, at the children playing with their propellers, sending them endlessly into the sky, catching them when they fell, launching them again. "I wonder if they know, the children."

"What," said the blind man, "could children possibly know?"

Ada put her arms around him, said, "Goodbye then."

"Perhaps," said he, "we shall see each other again before we are ash."

"Perhaps, Charlie." Ada fell in step with the crowds and walked away, straight forward, though the market, into the city.

Mitosis

Like a Christmas tree in a drug addict's holiday fantasy, Ellen Laurier's IV pole glistened and shined and promised. The bags, twinkling ornaments hung from shiny chrome branches, their contents liquefied presents, supplemented with the stocking-stuffer of handfuls and handfuls of pills. All told, she would be dead a dozen times over if she wasn't so used to the chemical delight. First the stocking stuffers: sumatriptan for the migraines caused by the pain medications, zofran and phenergan for the nausea, benadryl for the itching that so many drugs at once can cause. And then there were the big ones, the wishlist presents: the methadone and morphine and demerol and elavil, all which could dull the psychological as well as erase the physical pain that had coursed through her.

With seventeen admits in fifteen weeks, Ellen knew the drill.

The nurse, Eliza, who rigged the IV pole, stacking narcotics three deep, knew that this patient in room 6 was only there for the drugs. She had long enough to know this as surely as she knew that Doctor Albert was happier to manage his patients through a prescription pad, and still she felt badly for the girl. She would watch room 6 staring at the clock, waiting for the hands to align with the magic hour of next dose, and it was a look of such boredom, such longing, such need that Eliza's heart just broke. Besides, it was not her job to contradict, and when the venom hit then 6 would be out of her hair so she could get to her other patients. There was some guilt in this brushing off of the junkie for a moment's piece of mind, but she took her comfort in not having written the prescriptions, in not really knowing what kind of pain was happening. After all, she merely wanted to help people. And that poor girl didn't need any more judgement. She hung the IVs, set up the PCA pumps, locked the narcotics inside their tamper-resistant case, unwound and applied the tubing to the bags and to the IV, and to room 6.

*

The old oak tree, which Ellen and her twin sister Margaret had played on with all of their friends as children, was not given the same care, did not have the shiny metal pole to hold up its elixirs. Instead it was housed in a makeshift shed, a growth upon the side of their childhood home, which Margaret had erected after that first day Ellen was in the hospital, the tree split in half. There are no windows and the one door is kept locked. A sweat-hose coiled up the half-trunks and along the branches and through it ran a water and glucose solution, peppered with MiracleGro and life, if one could call it that. The sweat hose was fed by a hulking water reservoir and pump at the base. There was no more tire swing. There were no more children. No sun.

*

Every twelve hours, at seven, the bags line up. Doses scheduled for every two, three, four and six all land together, all unfurl their tendrils through the same bag of saline, all feed through the same pipeline to vein and heart. Ellen gets up, pushing along her mobile IV pole, and heads outside to smoke. Old hat. She shrugs off the sleep that is nearly induced so that she can be seen, so that family members lingering in the lobby away from their broken loved ones can gaze in wonder at the miracle of Ellen's drug cache. They have never seen someone so electric, she thinks, never seen someone so exotic.

They cannot help but stare. They wonder how this girl can even walk. They wonder if that is what will happen to grandma. They wonder if that will be them someday, if they will be that chained, that destroyed.

*

Should a tree be struck by lightning, chunks of bark and cork tissue would be sent flying in the explosion, torn from the trunk and major scaffold limbs, sent burning into the grass, smoldering and threatening to burn down the house, the neighborhood, the city. The water inside the cells would boil instantly. The DNA strands would unzip, but the RNA would be long dead, the ribosomes splintered, the thread of information burnt and destroyed and useless. The cell walls would dry or disintegrate or melt, the plasma membrane giving way, spilling what was left. The cells would die. The vascular tissues that ran the length of the wound would be interrupted and cauterized; the rays that ran the radius of the trunk would be so scorched that they would never again conduct fluid up the tree's cambrial structures under what was left of the bark. The root hairs that had extracted minerals from the ground would flame and combust and the tree would be left for a while without access to nutrients, and when the roots would re-grow, the whole process would be different, twisted, forever changed. The tree would do nothing for the woman smoldering on the ground.

*

Martin is only coming because Margaret asked, because she cannot stand to bear the hospital and her broken sister without him. He goes, though he can stand neither the location nor his fiancée's sister. He sees Ellen standing outside, grasping that thin chrome pole like it's her displaced spine, sucking nicotine out of a cigarette with the vigor a hurricane could rally for. Martin very briefly entertains the fantasy that Ellen will catch a cold that with her habits morphs into pneumonia and bronchitis and sepsis and ends with his arm around Margaret at the addict's funeral, holding his fiancée's hand and telling her that she will get through it and he will take care of her.

He shakes his head and chastises himself. He pulls off his wool overcoat and sidles up to Ellen and drapes her like an empress. "What are you doing out here?" The question is ridiculous, but so is she in her thin gray hospital gown fastened with only a few meager strings of cotton tie in the kind of cold that instantly pierces through his dress shirt and under like nothing.

Ellen looks at Martin, coldly, pulling again from the filter—how many milligrams are in a puff, or a dozen puffs? How many in a cigarette? What is her dosage now and can she add it to the list she carries in her head? She rummages in the pocket of her thin gown for something solid to hold onto. "I'm smoking," she finally says in a dull rasp. He has materialized from out of the mist of her wandering mind and she just wishes that he would leave forever with his blue pinstripe pants and red tie flapping in the wind; he probably thinks he dresses roguishly. "I'm smoking a cigarette."

Martin just nods. In his right hand is a briefcase filled with the words habeas and allegedly, with stacks of notes for future motions. With his left he gathers up his coat with Ellen inside and coerces the bulk back indoors. "You'll catch cold. Come on."

Ellen complies. Despite the objections welling in her, she is powerless at this moment, unable to explain why she must replace the oxygen in her lungs with this blackness that comes in such convenient packaging, to be exhaled with a sigh into the world and a billowing dull flowering of dead fire that she can imagine is her life, burnt and smoldering, escaping from inside.

*

A tree can survive for a time in total darkness. Not everyone is aware of this. Everyone knows about photosynthesis, about the green of leaves and the chloroplasts that turn light into life. They do not know that chloroplasts convert photon energy into glucose derivatives that funnel through and fuel the tree. What they couldn't imagine is that a little sugar solution in the water can bypass this entirely. Goodbye sun, you unnecessary shining. Up through the phloem, through roots and branches, this solution will make its way through remaining cell walls and the tree will live and will grow in its total, secret, darkness.

*

Margaret strides in the room glowing with irritation. "Martin tells me you were outside smoking."

Ellen smiles from her bed at her healthy mirror image, forgetting how much she's changed. She waves her hand, admires the IV tubing taped to the back of her palm. She pushes the call button on her bed.

"What do you need?"

"It's almost time for my meds," Ellen says, "I don't want my nurse to forget. Anyways, why would I be outside smoking? He probably saw someone else."

"Someone else?" Margaret curls her mouth downwards and drops the lids of her eyes. Defeated. She is tired of scolding her sister. How do you go from perfect copy, from companion and confidant, to ward and obligation? "Ellen, you're going to get even sicker. You're supposed to get better."

"I'm fine," Ellen waves her off with small, distracted circles. "I'm in a hospital, they can treat it. A pill and boom, all better."

"Just work on what you have, don't try gathering new diseases. This isn't a scavenger hunt." She sees her sister still waving her hands, still lost in some small mercy of forgetfulness. "You're high. I'll come back later."

"Me?" Ellen scrunches up her face like a child. Imagines herself a child and how she used to be able to play off her mother. She mime counts the bags on the IV pole. "Not high, just dopey." She smiles.

*

Confused at its unusual state of affairs, a tree in the dark will accelerate, become unpredictable. If it could climb higher and higher, perhaps it could push through and find the light, past whatever blocks the sun. Until then, though, the tree is blind, accelerating through the haze with barely any idea of where up even is, or how much further it must go to reach the threshold. Usually, should a tree be covered completely enough for the sun to be so absent it would die before it could find its way out.

*

Dr. Albert skulks up on Margaret in the hallway, waiting until he is almost near enough to touch before he calls her name. There is something intoxicating about her. Perhaps because he has seen so much of her alternate reality.

Margaret turns with redness in the corners of her eyes and a fierce determination. "What's wrong with her? Is there something else wrong, is that why she keeps ending up," and she lets her eyes dart a little upward and leaves the conversation to flutter down the hall. She holds her breath and finds comfort in the gesture, a small nod of suffering, her body slowly asking and begging for air, as if it can somehow parallel her twin sister being struck by lightning.

"No." Dr. Albert dismisses it with a wave of his hand and a genial smile. He doesn't want to upset her, this delicate fern. "Things actually seem to be progressing quite well. Her external wounds are completely healed, no more swelling, no infections. The scarring on her foot where the lightning passed is very minimal, so it shouldn't impede her. Her EKG came back normal. She's come a long way in the last six months."

Margaret nods and breaths. "Why is she in so much pain?" Just dopey. "We keep talking about her progress, but then I come here and—it doesn't always seem like such great progress is all."

"It's difficult to say," Dr. Albert buys a little time to construct the thoughts he can share. "I wouldn't want to hazard a guess. Being struck by lightning is, uh, it's very traumatic. It's a very big incident for your body. It disrupts the entire nervous system, permanently changing a lot of the pathways of the nerves, new paths, new ways to process, and maybe killing some. What I'm saying is that it makes the body feel new, and it can take some time to adjust. It could be some time still. Or maybe there's something we're missing. Has she been favoring an arm, touching an exit wound, anything like that?"

Margaret things of anything that might help, enough that she feels her face sliding into her mother's frown. There is Ellen's moodiness, they have been fighting constantly. They no longer look alike. What she had understood to be the world was slipping and slipping. Was Ellen limping? Could she have missed something like that, off in her own spiral of doubt and missing something like that? She has nothing to say, nothing to proffer and so she finds herself blurting before her hands can stop her lips, "she's been moody lately."

"Well," Dr. Albert says with what he hopes is not a patronizing tone, and takes the opportunity to lay his hand on Margaret's shoulder. "We've adjusted her medications a bit, which should help with irritability. When you're in pain, it's easy to lash out." Ellen lashed out earlier for forty five minutes straight until he caved and upped the morphine from 4mg, so she would let him leave the room for some peace and quiet.

"Did you increase it again?"

"She was in a lot of pain." Dr. Albert can feel how

weakly he offers this. He sees Margaret's face drop, her eyes dull.

"I sometimes think she's faking," Margaret offers. "She seems to get around fine, she walks around, when she isn't too high, she leaves the house. She's just so moody, so easy to disturb. I don't understand why she isn't getting better."

Dr. Albert hesitates while he searches for the answer that will ease her fears, assure her of his competence, build whatever the hell it is that needs to be built and he can't quite figure out. He can't tell her that he'd write Ellen into a coma some days if it'd get her to shut up, or that he is happiest when she is gone from the hospital. Perhaps it is a flaw of his, perhaps he isn't patient enough, caring enough, but there are so many addicts, so many whiners, so many people with real complaints too, and so much pain and suffering that you— "Pain is something we can't measure for someone else. People deal in different ways. We only know what we are told for other people, and it isn't my job to guess, to make her suffer because I grew skeptical of an otherwise exemplary young woman."

"Just give me something to do." Margaret sees this man as a good man, if not a great one. A doctor who is helping, an expert who just has to ponder the question for long enough that he will figure out what to fill her hands with, what to ease into her life so that she can fix Ellen.

"Just keep an eye on her. If she is reacting to something, let us know. Maybe you can catch something we don't get to see, or maybe this all just resolves itself." He is getting to her, but he doesn't know what else to say. "And if you're really worried, maybe talk to her about easing back on the good days, talk her through it, but don't push her."

"Thank you," Margaret says. He said it twice: work itself out. Like this was a phase, like Ellen was a teenager with a tantrum. "I appreciate it."

*

By nature, trees seek out the sun, grow towards it. Phototropic. Most have seen examples of this, a tree grown oddly out of the side of a hill will curve, bending up towards the light. With no light, there would be no guidance as to how it should grow. The tree would lose its internal clock, begin to grow madly, uncertain. Gibberellin would become unevenly distributed, here on the right side, here on the left side, causing the cells to elongate in unusual patterns, making the trunk lean to the west, to the east, to the north, straightening up again for a few inches, curving back eastward towards the house. The trunk would grow thinner, brittle, exerting all of its energy to escaping the darkness. Auxin would continue to flow from the tip of the tree, nourished by water and glucose, caressed in the darkness and told to grow if only God knew where.

*

When she is home again, Ellen stares out of her window into the bleak night. She recites the clichés of home to herself. Where you lay your head at night. Family. Where the heart is. Sure. Home is where you listen to the house contracting in the cold, creaking and cracking as it pulls against nails and screws and yet more straining wood and you nearly sob with the shock of memories best left unremembered.

Outside, she used to see branches of the tree wagging in the wind, waving slender leafed fingers at her. Now there is only the cloudy sky and the hulking shame of plywood housing built around the tree. She tries on a ring that was never hers, she slips it off. She will never wear it, but it is a comfort. It is poor comfort. She needs a smoke.

Margaret is in the kitchen, washing dishes in her robe while the smell of freshly baking bread conquers the senses, filling everything with warmth. Ellen looks around for her pills, decides to delay her smoke a bit. "Hey."

Margaret cranes her neck, pauses in her dishes. "Hey yourself."

"What are you making?" Ellen pours a glass of water and grabs the bottle of Elavil, sitting down at the small breakfast table. She thumbs dumbly through a copy of *Time*. She never felt uncomfortable talking to her twin before the accident. Things are changing.

"Cranberry orange. Should be done in an hour or so." Margaret is unsure if she should finish the dishes or sit at the table. Is Ellen just moving through, or is she staying for a minute more? She's hardly around for long anymore, always moving, always gone, never in one place unless she's sleeping.

"I feel so transient," Ellen closes the magazine she spent all of thirty seconds rifling through, shakes a few pills out and swallows. "I'm sorry."

"How many is that?"

"One." Ellen wishes she had the IV at home so she could feel it immediately, like in the hospital, not waiting for the pill to dissolve, not having to answer banal questions about numbers. She would grind and snort the chalky pill, but not ever in front of Margaret. She doesn't have any heroin in the house, though it is an appealing thought. She only has these two stupid pills. Three.

Margaret sets aside the dishes, shakes the water off her hands and dries them on her robe. "What's up?" She takes a seat and it almost feels like before.

"I died," Ellen says and the memory is instantly on her.

It wasn't raining yet. The cumulonimbus clouds were so beautiful; tumultuous towers in the sky, harmless looking when they weren't directly overhead. But then, lightning didn't need to be directly above. She remembers seeing the bolt coming her way exactly as it hit her, the image burned into her retina, the pain in her shoulder, like being stabbed with fire, the pain in her foot, the smell of burning hair and burning cloth and melting rubber as the lightning found its way out through her foot, through her sock, through her shoe, to the ground. She remembers the sound reverberating in her chest and the sight of the tree, also struck, splitting in two, the trunk peeling apart from itself, the chunks of bark that hit her as she was falling. She remembers waking up in the hospital, the words V-fib, asystole, residual deficits, Lichtenberg figures. Pain. "And I came back."

"I know," Margaret was there; she heard the explosion, the crack of the tree and the groaning of the wood and the cry of pain. She gave her twin sister CPR through her tears, she ran into the house through the sudden rain where her phone lay, she called the ambulance through sobs, she waited in the ED for years and years, and she remembers the doctors telling her the words quivering of the heart and flatline and residual deficits and scarring and pain.

She doesn't know, Ellen thinks. She doesn't know what it's like to feel parts of your body boil. She doesn't know what it feels like for all of your hair to suddenly be charged and stand on end and burn off. She doesn't know what your eyes feel like when they shake so hard and hot that you are blind to the world with your lids wide open. She doesn't know what it feels like for your heart to be stopped and restarted. She doesn't know what it feels like to imagine that there is lightning still inside of her, maybe it didn't all exit through her foot, and maybe it will manifest itself and kill her. She doesn't know what it's like to feel terror every time you get a static electricity shock, convinced that it is the end.

"I feel electric," Ellen says to fill the silence; her words sound rushed to her ears, desperate, "like the lightning has given me a sense of urgency." She drums her fingers on the table. "I'm nervous all of the time, anxious. It's hard to concentrate. I want to go back to work; I want to have somewhere to be every day like you do."

"You said you couldn't concentrate. What good are you in a lab with trembling hands?"

"I go crazy here.'

Margaret shifts her weight in the absence of something helpful to say. She thinks about reaching for her sister's hand, but she can't bring herself to do it, she still feels too distant; she folds them in her lap instead. "Where do you go when you leave? Sometimes you're gone all day."

"Nowhere really," Ellen says. "Sometimes I go to the bookstore, or the coffee shop." Sometimes to the pawnshop; sometimes to the underpass on Langston Ave. "Sometimes I go look at dresses. Out."

"I just worry. It makes me feel like mom, but when I come home and you're gone, and you don't come back for hours I just know that you are dead. That the lightning has caught you again, and I wasn't there, and it is all my fault."

"The resting is bad enough already. I have to walk, I have to be away from here. I have to get away from that terrible tree."

"Remember when mom and dad used to push us in the old tire swing? Remember when we used to climb it every day?"

"Of course."

"I just don't want anything to happen to it. It's all we have left of mom and dad. I can't give that up."

Ellen let's herself lean forward and put her hand on Margaret's. But something in the touch feels wrong and she pulls it off, lets it lie limp in the middle of the table, then retracts it. Something wells inside of her that she didn't know was there, and she is suddenly crying. Margaret doesn't understand. She can't. She wasn't struck. She didn't lie in the hospital for weeks, almost being dead. She didn't need the liter of pain medications to balance even, the second liter to forget, the continued presence to feel normal. Margaret doesn't need a chemical aid to lie still for five minutes and she doesn't get high to forget that things can never go back. She doesn't understand anything.

"I'm sorry," Margaret says. "I don't understand what you're going through. I know. I just want to help." Margaret reaches for Ellen's shoulder. "Maybe you can help me with the tree. Maybe we can do it together. Like a project."

Ellen nods. She touches her hair. It is shorter than Margaret's and darker. She has been losing weight. She can see in her sister the slightest plumping of the cheeks, the healthy glow of the living. "I miss looking alike. I miss having a me that was not me."

Margaret looks at her sister, at her jittery eyes, at the

lines. She is jealous of her sister's weight loss but glad she didn't go through it. She resents the difference between them as well.

They sit in silence and try to be content in it. Things aren't different, they tell themselves, just hard.

"I'm gonna go grab a smoke," Ellen finally announces.

"At least put a coat on," Margaret says. It is a concession.

"I'm fine," Ellen says, and is gone, into the cold.

Margaret watches Ellen through the window, arms wrapped around her frail body and smoking.

*

Confused, blind, fed by sugar and deprived of the sun, the cells in the oak tree would reproduce rapidly. Cytokinin would flood through the plasma membrane, reaching the nucleus, signaling the buildup of energy and material; prophase meant the shrinking of chromosomes, wound tight and tense. Then the cell walls would dissolve and the dam would be broken. The centromeres would line up to be snagged by the spindle fibers of metaphase, to be pulled apart, torn, divided during anaphase, the walls being built up again for renewal in telophase, the chromosomes finally relaxed, to begin to breathe easy: a new life would be built. The new cells would elongate and divide again. A hundred million times over this cytokinesis.

*

A knock on the door wakes Ellen. She didn't remember falling asleep on the couch but there you go. It's Martin at the door, but she opens up anyways, gives him a "hey" and walks away, leaving the door open for him to shut behind himself. In the kitchen she opens a bottle of morphine, fishes one out and washes it down with gulping draughts of water. It's a little after 10pm.

"I wake you?" Martin comes into the kitchen, wearing a black shirt and a red tie that he feels gives him a strength he often doubts. Ellen nods yes with the miserable bleariness of the hungover, but offers no words. "I guess Margaret isn't home yet?"

"I didn't know she was gone."

Martin squirms a little, realizing that he may have given away too much, that Ellen will be able to detect his deception like a drug dog, that she will intuit everything. "She's worried about you," he finally manages. "You're on a lot of drugs."

"I'm in a lot of pain." Ellen slips her hands into her pockets and locks her eyes defiantly with his. She fingers the metal there. It is solid and reminds her that she is solid too. She lets her body feel how solid everything is.

"Do you ever think, I don't know." And in that moment he doesn't know. He knows what he had planned to say and he knows that it is foolishness to utter, that it comes from a place which is neither knowledgeable nor kind, that it is a thought without a home, that it should be smothered that it should be destroyed. But it is too late. "The medications really add up. Do you wonder how long you'll be on them?"

Ellen fiddles with the empty glass. "That's what doctors and insurance is for. And Margaret helps with the money." Ellen bounces her feet. "It's the least she can do. She called my boss. Did you know that? Asking her not to let me come back before I was better. Can you believe that?" Ellen lets her gaze drift over to Martin again, at his suit, at the briefcase filled with guilty and unlucky names and regrets that she has spoken of it at all, of her frustrations with her sister. It feels a betrayal. "I don't really feel like talking about it. I'm sure Margaret will be home soon."

"Ellen," Martin is feeling defensive of his fiancée, and he can't let Ellen leave with a jab at Margaret's protective instinct. "Margaret was looking for your mother's old wedding band. She wants it for the wedding. Know where it is?" Ellen doesn't flinch, and Martin isn't sure if this is the sign of innocence or a great liar, or if it is only the apathy of the doped and the barely listening.

"Goodnight," Ellen says as she stands to make it to her bed before the morphine really hits, because it makes her feel, almost always, tired like a soul that has wandered the planes of limbo for far too long.

"Why don't you like me?"

Martin's question, devoid of context, sans preamble, not probing, but actively seeking, flies through her. She feels herself turn as if a third party to her body's actions. "You met Margaret at my parents' funeral. At their funeral. We were grieving a tragic car crash and you were picking up chicks. But I got over that. It's been four years, you can let some things go. You helped us move into our old house, you were cute together. M&M. I was just happy for her. Then, when I was in the hospital for what, a week? Still dazed, still barely holding on, you proposed to her. What kind of a creep does that? Are you turned on by tragedy?" And this was beside him stealing away her mirror image, leaving only the shadow version lingering in the borders of the mirror.

"Everything was planned," Martin protests. "Everything. The ring, the reservations, the band. For months. I didn't jump at the opportunity for more tragedy. Besides, I hoped it would cheer her up." He wishes that last sentence didn't come out. It turns his stomach. It is a story he has told dozens of times, of violin's and jewelry hidden in desert. How cheesy, how cute. He always leaves out how distracted Margaret was, how much he regretted asking her then with her sister hooked up to a breathing machine. He tries to simply forget seeing her later that night, her back turned, fingering the ring and whispering that at least she wouldn't have to be alone.

"You're a fucking creep."

"That's not fair."

Fair or not, Ellen is done. She is already halfway up the stairs.

*

The tree would know. It would know its death was imminent. That it must escape or die. Its erratic energy would have been wasted, for naught, if it couldn't get through. So it would grow faster and taller, more crooked and more unusual, spreading its mass through the black chamber, aging faster than ever before. Ethylene is released, causing abscission layers on the leaf stems, cascading them through the black air to the black grass. With light gone, so too would be photorespiration and all that could remain would be mitochondrial dark respiration. Inside of the tree, in its being, cells would die, leaving only the husk of their walls to become xylem, to transport the sweet laden water, to feed the tree, to let it grow still more quickly, ever more perversely, and over the months it would press itself into the side of the house.

*

A noise wakes Ellen. She sits up and listens to the creaking of the wood in the old house, groaning and pushing and shoving against more wood. She reaches for a bottle of—what time is it? It doesn't matter because there are no bottles there. It doesn't matter. She can't find them in the kitchen either. Well. She'll have a smoke.

At the door, Margaret and Martin are fiddling with the final touches of a lock that requires a key on each side, which she knows she will never possesses.

Margaret looks up and panics, adopts a bright smile. "Hey, what's up?"

Ellen tilts her head wildly to the side, in a parody of how her sister lilts when she lies. "What's up? What's up? Oh, not much, just getting locked away in our own goddamned house. What's up with you?"

Margaret shrinks back, losing the nerve she'd had when she suggested this, sliding into Martin's arms who already wishes he had protested the move. She was certain, still is, except for the uncertainty.

"Well?" Ellen flings her arms wide around her. Drops them to her side with a clap, like thunder. "Is this where my fucking pills are? Is this your plan, torture and imprisonment? Then I'll be better? Are you two insane?"

"The doctor said you're better." Margaret feels herself stepping forward like a martyr. "He doesn't know why you need so much. He said it's best if we wean you off of them." And as she says it, it feels so much like the truth that it becomes it. She will never remember that she took the words and twisted the top off. She just wants to help.

"So you just took all of them? Not a very progressive step, is it? Who the hell are you to decide that? I was the one who was struck. I am the one who is dying. Do you remember this?"

"Ellen, calm down," Margaret says.

Behind the anger, Ellen feels her breathing grow difficult. She is more trapped than she has ever been. In this husk of a body, in this house. She blinks her eyes, she flexes her hands, feeling adrenaline. "Calm? Yeah, just calm down. Accept your imprisonment."

"The doctor said you should stay inside and rest. You shouldn't be disappearing all day. You shouldn't be smoking at 1am in your pajamas. I've been too lenient. I realize that now. I just let you keep getting worse. I let you wander, I didn't keep you safe. I let you pile on pill after pill, slipping farther and farther away. It's my fault."

"What are you talking about? What if there is a fire, Margaret?" For some reason, the adrenaline is already waning. There is something else instead, something colder.

"I'll be there with you. I don't want to lose you. You've been drifting. You're destroying yourself. You leave stoned, you come home stoned, you eat narcotics and barely anything else."

"Margaret."

"It's my fault. I know it. I already lost mom and dad. Now I'm losing you, and you're attacking Martin. He told me what you said about our engagement, he told me how you want him gone, that you want me to be alone, that you don't want us to be together so that you can punish me because you were outside by the tree waiting for me and I was taking too long getting ready. And you stole mom's ring and probably sold it for drugs. You're probably sharing needles. God."

It occurs to Martin that he's missing something, even now. It occurs to Margaret that she should have done this long ago. The doctors could patch up a wound but their usefulness ended there. It was up to her to salvage this family.

"Get out." Ellen says. "Get away from me."

"No."

Ellen withdraws the ring from her pocket where she has kept it clasped in a hand she didn't even realize was a fist. She holds it in front of her sister and is angry and tired and spent. Margaret snatches it.

"You didn't sell it yet." Margaret accuses.

"Of course not. I needed something to hold onto. Give me my pills back, Margaret. You can't keep me in here like you have with the tree. I'm not your science experiment."

"The tree is safe." And every day, when she locks herself in and shines a light up the shattered trunk, it looks taller, it looks bigger. It is a confirmation of her rightness: you can't argue with results. "Remember when we grew up on that tree? I'm saving it."

Martin makes a noise of support. Shuffles.

"Give me my pills, Margaret."

"I'm saving you."

When Margaret turns her back and gestures to Martin that they should go, Ellen feels herself rushing forward, she feels the words erupting. "Where the hell do you think you're going?"

Margaret turns and slaps her sister. It hurts her hand. "You wanted us gone. Fine. It'll give you some time to think."

Ellen is finally actually awake. She is finally fully aware of what is happening. Her cheek burns, her mind riles, but she can still only stare in bottled rage while Martin stares apologetically and then is shuffled out of the house, as Margaret says something self-righteous and locks the door behind her.

All of the doors are locked in the same way, the front door resounds with the final bolt turned. Ellen can feel the lightning all through her body. She can feel it in her shoulder and out through her leg. She takes a shower, wipes away the fog on the mirror with her hand, staring at the beautiful dendrite scarring that etches down her back. She can still feel it burning.

A part of her understands. She pours a few whiskeys, three fingers at a time until her esophagus burns more than her bones. In the morning, Margaret will come with apologies and croissants. She will relent on the doors, she will explain the attitude and Ellen will nod and will understand. She will take the pills back and feel them slowly erase the static that is building and building and burning her up. They will go to the hospital together the next time it grows too much to handle, Margaret will get married and Ellen will stand with her, and Martin will be forgiven his poor timing upon poor timing. This is because Ellen knows that family is what matters. It has mattered her whole life, since she and Margaret came out as duplicates, and all the way until they grew into strangers.

Ellen tries all of the doors one more time. They are locked, but the windows aren't. None of them.

*

The tree would reach the edge of the house; the unnatural growth that had spanned the gap until it nestled into the corner that met the roof. It would push. It would not show any signs of stopping. The cells would still divide, would still elongate, the Gibberellin still flowing, the Auxin still running. The tree, with the last of its brittle strength, pushes into the house, upwards and eastwards, stretching the siding and the framing against screws and nails and insulation. The roof separates from the frame. The siding cracked, falling in places, staying in others. It grows faster through the darkness, pushing higher. The roof tilts higher on its axis, a full degree, two degrees, pulling more nails and more boards until it reaches apex, until it is almost completely separated from the rest of the house. It perches there, a precarious point, threatening to break in the middle, to crash back down on top of the house, to pancake the floors below until there is only dust and splinters and a black, fractured tree that will grow and grow and grow forever. The sound of the stress is intense.

What is Missing, What is Left

I can't stand ghost hunters, though they mean well. Most of them. They certainly don't do it for the money. I'm no expert on the subject, but I listen to them sometimes, as they sit in dark rooms with their bowls of water and electronic doodads. They whisper about how they're going to make rent, and what it really means to be in love. They wonder aloud why the dead linger. Sometimes the equipment will screech or beep and everyone will get excited for a little while, but mostly they sit and wait, whispering, as if ghosts are spooked by loud noises, or maybe they think ghosts can't hear them if they whisper. It's not true. I hear everything, and shouting doesn't bother me at all.

What drives me nuts about the ghost hunters are their questions. They're so dumb. They ask if I'm happy where I am. They ask me what I want. I try to tell them. The password for the router is Rj2939abiO. I want them to pass this along to my husband. I don't know how the hell he managed to reset his wifi settings in the first place, but he did, and he can't figure out how to log in again. He's a good man, and no one deserves to be forced to live without the internet.

The ghost hunters ask if I have unfinished business. As if that means anything. I had a life I was trying to live, for whatever that's worth. I hadn't ever lined the liquor cabinet, and now there are whisky bottle shaped stains in the wood. My husband and I had never really apologized after a big fight; we just stormed off and then eventually moved on with our lives as if it never happened. I hadn't gotten around to a life insurance policy. Not that this was unfinished business anymore, not really. I have the song from the Simpsons movie stuck in my head. Perhaps that's unfinished business. Perhaps that is what I need to purge to move on. You know the song, where Spider Pig does whatever a spider pig does.

God help me, Homer J. Simpson may have been the most important voice of my generation. Not important as in, having something to say. Important as in: people actually listened. Is that unfinished business or just a tragedy?

I have moved through the streets, alone, walking through the crowds and through the people and the walls. I have seen their intimate moments and I have thought, why am I here? I've looked for other ghosts, but I haven't found any. I don't know if this means that they don't exist, or if we are all doomed to our own personal haunts.

The ghost hunters tell my husband that I'm not there. Not here. There is no sign of me. I'm not haunting our house. Frauds. I watch my husband break down in our house without wifi. I watch him that evening as he picks up a picture of us: it's years old, we never really took that many pictures, and he holds it close to his face. He begins to talk to the picture, to the ghost-me that is not the me who is this ghost.

He says: "It's not enough for me to say that I miss you. It's you who are missing from me, like a limb." He weeps on the couch, and says he cannot be whole without me.

Which is more than he said when we were alive, and I would tell him that, but probably he already knows, and really, that's not why I'm here. I'm here to give him that damned password, and so I wait for him to buy a Ouija board so I can tell him, tell him that I love him, that I always did, and that the password is Rj2939abiO.

Acknowledgments

Many of these stories originally appeared in a slightly different form in a number of literary journals: "Now or Never or Later" in *Southwest Review*, "Pillars of Thorns" and "The Boxes" in *Juked*, "Goat Sucker" in *Lunch Ticket*, "Re Member" in *Rawboned*, "Memory is an Elephant" in *Far Enough East*, "Mitosis" in *Kaaterskill Basin*, "What is Missing, What is Left" in *Marathon Literary Review*, "Body, Etc." in *The Notre Dame Review*.

"Like Water," and "Startled Poet Who is a Bat" were made possible by the generosity of the Taft-Nicholson Center and grants by the Lawrence T. & Janet T. Dee foundation.

None of these stories would have been possible without the love, assistance, belief, and support from Jenn Daniels, Michelle Donahue, Stephen Graham Jones, Melanie Rae Thon, Joe Sacksteader, Molly Gaudry, Rhett Cooper, Mat Johnson, Alexander Parsons, and Lance Olsen, among many others. Thank you.

JI Daniels has an MFA from the University of Houston, is currently a PhD Candidate at the University of Utah, and is the author of the novel *Mount Fugue*, as well as short works appearing in *Notre Dame Review*, *Southwest Review*, *Diagram*, and elsewhere.

www.ingramcontent.com/pod-product-compliance
Lightning Source LLC
Chambersburg PA
CBHW010349170726
48284CB00011B/2852